QUIET DAYS
IN
CLICHY

Other works by Henry Miller
Published by Grove Press

Black Spring

The Rosy Crucifixion:
Sexus, Plexus, Nexus

Tropic of Cancer

Tropic of Capricorn

Moloch

Crazy Cock

Under the Roofs of Paris

HENRY MILLER

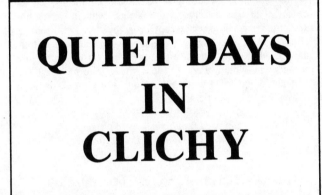

QUIET DAYS
IN
CLICHY

GROVE PRESS • NEW YORK

Published simultaneously in Canada
Printed in the United States of America

Library of Congress Cataloging-in-Publication Data

Miller, Henry, 1891–1980
Quiet days in Clichy.

I. Title.
PS3525.I5454Q5 1987   813'.52   87-12377
ISBN 0-8021-3016-X

Grove Press
841 Broadway
New York, NY 10003

02   20 19 18 17 16 15 14 13 12 11

As I write, night is falling and people are going to dinner. It's been a gray day, such as one often sees in Paris. Walking around the block to air my thoughts, I couldn't help but think of the tremendous contrast between the two cities (New York and Paris). It is the same hour, the same sort of day, and yet even the word gray, which brought about the association, has little in common with that *gris* which, to the ears of a Frenchman, is capable of evoking a world of thought and feeling. Long ago, walking the streets of Paris, studying the watercolors on exhibit in the shop windows, I was aware of the singular absence of what is known as Payne's gray. I mention it because Paris, as everyone knows, is pre-eminently a gray city. I mention it because, in the realm of watercolor, American painters use this made-to-order gray excessively and obsessively. In France the range of grays is seemingly infinite; here the very effect of gray is lost.

I was thinking of this immense world of gray which I knew in Paris because at this hour, when ordinarily I would be strolling towards the boulevards, I find myself eager to return home and write: a complete reversal of my normal habits. There my day would be over, and I would instinctively set out to mingle with the crowd. Here the crowd, empty of all color, all nuance, all distinction, drives me in on myself, drives me back to my room, to seek in my imagination those elements of a now missing life which, when blended and assimilated, may again produce the soft natural grays so necessary to the creation of a sustained, harmonious existence. Looking towards the Sacré Cœur from any point along the Rue Laffitte on a day like this, an hour like this, would be sufficient to put me in ecstasy. It has had that effect upon me even when I was hungry and had no place to sleep. Here, even if I had a thousand dollars in my pocket, I know of no sight which could arouse in me the feeling of ecstasy.

On a gray day in Paris I often found myself walking towards the Place Clichy in Montmartre. From Clichy to Aubervilliers there is a long string of cafés, restaurants, theaters, cinemas, haberdashers, hotels and bordels. It is the Broadway of Paris corresponding to that little stretch between 42nd and 53rd Streets. Broadway is fast, dizzying, dazzling, and no place to sit down. Montmartre is sluggish, lazy, indifferent, somewhat shabby and seedy-looking, not glamorous so much as seductive, not scintillating but glowing with a smoldering flame. Broadway looks exciting, even magical at times, but there is no fire, no heat— it is a brilliantly illuminated asbestos display, the paradise of advertising agents. Montmartre is worn, faded, derelict, nakedly vicious, mercenary, vulgar. It is, if anything, repellent rather than attractive, but insidiously repellent, like vice itself. There are little bars filled almost exclusively with whores, pimps, thugs and gamblers, which, no matter if you pass them up a thousand times, finally suck you in and claim you as a victim. There are hotels in the side streets leading off the boulevard whose ugliness is so sinister that you shudder at the thought of entering them, and yet it is inevitable that you will one day pass a night, perhaps a week or a month, in one of them. You may even become so attached to the place as to find one day that your whole life has been transformed and that what you once regarded as sordid, squalid, miserable, has now become charming, tender, beautiful. This insidious charm of Montmartre is due, in large part, I suspect, to the unconcealed traffic in sex. Sex is not romantic, particularly when it is commercialized, but it does create an aroma, pungent and nostalgic, which is far more glamorous and seductive than the most brilliantly illuminated Gay White Way. In fact it is obvious enough that the sexual life flourishes better in a dim, murky light: it is at home in the chiaroscuro and not in the glare of the neon light.

At one corner of the Place Clichy is the

Café Wepler, which was for a long period my favorite haunt. I have sat there inside and out at all times of the day in all kinds of weather. I knew it like a book. The faces of the waiters, the managers, the cashiers, the whores, the clientele, even the attendants in the lavatory, are engraved in my memory as if they were illustrations in a book which I read every day. I remember the first day I entered the Café Wepler, in the year 1928, with my wife in tow; I remember the shock I experienced when I saw a whore fall dead drunk across one of the little tables on the terrace and nobody ran to her assistance. I was amazed and horrified by the stoical indifference of the French; I still am, despite all the good qualities in them which I have since come to know. *"It's nothing, it was just a whore . . . she was drunk."* I can still hear those words. Even today they make me shudder. But it is very French, this attitude, and, if you don't learn to accept it, your stay in France won't be very pleasant.

On the gray days, when it was chilly everywhere except in the big cafés, I looked forward with pleasure to spending an hour or two at the Café Wepler before going to dinner. The rosy glow which suffused the place emanated from the cluster of whores who usually congregated near the entrance. As they gradually distributed themselves among the clientele, the place became not only warm and rosy but fragrant. They fluttered about in the dimming light like perfumed fireflies. Those who had not been fortunate enough to find a customer would saunter slowly out to the street, usually to return in a little while and resume their old places. Others swaggered in, looking fresh and ready for the evening's work. In the corner where they usually congregated it was like an exchange, the sex market, which has its ups and downs like other exchanges. A rainy day was usually a good day, it seemed to me. There are only two things you can do on a rainy day, as the saying goes, and the whores never wasted time playing cards.

It was in the late afternoon of a rainy day that I espied a newcomer at the Café Wepler. I had been out shopping, and my arms were loaded with books and phonograph records. I must have received an unexpected remittance from America that day because, despite the purchases I had made, I still had a few hundred francs in my pocket. I sat down near the place of exchange, surrounded by a bevy of hungry, itching whores whom I had no difficulty whatever in eluding because my eyes were fastened on this ravishing beauty who was sitting apart in a far corner of the café. I took her to be an attractive young woman who had made a rendezvous with her lover and who had come ahead of time perhaps. The *apéritif* which she had ordered had hardly been touched. At the men who passed her table she gave a full, steady glance, but that indicated nothing—a Frenchwoman doesn't avert her glance as does the English or the American woman. She looked around quietly, appraisingly, but without obvious effort to attract attention. She was discreet and dignified, thoroughly poised and self-contained. She was waiting. I too was waiting. I was curious to see whom she was waiting for. After a half hour, during which time I caught her eye a number of times and held it, I made up my mind that she was waiting for anyone who would make the proper overture. Ordinarily one has only to give a sign with the head or the hand and the girl will leave her table and join you—if she's that kind of girl. I was not absolutely sure even yet. She looked too good to me, too sleek, too well—nurtured, I might say.

When the waiter came round again I pointed her out and asked him if he knew her. When he said no I suggested that he invite her to come over and join me. I watched her face as he delivered the message. It gave me quite a thrill to see her smile and look my way with a nod of recognition. I expected her to get up immediately and come over, but instead she remained seated and smiled again, more discreetly this time, whereupon she turned her head away and appeared to gaze out the window dreamily. I allowed a few moments to intervene and then, seeing that she had no intention of making a move, I rose and walked over to her table. She greeted me cordially enough, quite as if I were a friend indeed, but I noticed that she was a little flustered, almost embarrassed. I wasn't sure whether she wanted me to sit down or not, but I sat down nevertheless and, after ordering drinks, quickly engaged her in conversation. Her voice was even more thrilling than her smile; it was well—pitched, rather low, and throaty. It was the voice of a woman who is glad to be alive, who indulges herself, who is careless and indigent, and who will do anything to preserve the modicum of freedom which she possesses. It was the voice of a giver, of a spender; its appeal went to the diaphragm rather than the heart.

I was surprised, I must confess, when she hastened to explain to me that I had made a *faux pas* in coming over to her table. "I thought you had understood," she said, "that I would join you outside. That's what I was trying to tell you telegraphically." She intimated that she did not want to be known here as a professional. I apologized for the blunder and offered to withdraw, which she accepted as a delicate gesture to be ignored by a squeeze of the hand and a gracious smile.

"What are all these things?" she said,

quickly changing the subject by pretending to be interested in the packages which I had placed on the table.

"Just books and records," I said, implying that they would hardly interest her.

"Are they French authors?" she asked, suddenly injecting a note of genuine enthusiasm, it seemed to me.

"Yes," I replied, "but they are rather dull, I fear. Proust, Céline, Elie Faure . . . You'd prefer Maurice Dekobra, no?"

"Let me see them, please. I want to see what kind of French books an American reads."

I opened the package and handed her the Elie Faure. It was *The Dance over Fire and Water*. She riffled the pages, smiling, making little exclamations as she read here and there. Then she deliberately put the book down, closed it, and put her hand over it as if to keep it closed. "Enough, let us talk about something more interesting." After a moment's silence, she added: "*Celui-là, est-il vraiment français?*"

"*Un vrai de vrai,*" I replied, with a broad grin.

She seemed puzzled. "It's excellent

French," she went on, as if to herself, "and yet it's not French either . . . *Comment dirais-je?*"

I was about to say that I understood perfectly when she threw herself back against the cushion, took hold of my hand and, with a roguish smile which was meant to reinforce her candor, said: "Look, I am a thoroughly lazy creature. I haven't the patience to read books. It's too much for my feeble brain."

"There are lots of other things to do in life," I answered, returning her smile. So saying, I placed my hand on her leg and squeezed it warmly. In an instant her hand covered mine, removed it to the soft, fleshy part. Then, almost as quickly, she drew my hand away with an—"*Assez, nous ne sommes pas seuls ici.*"

We sipped our drinks and relaxed. I was in no hurry to rush her off. For one thing, I was too enchanted by her speech, which was distinctive and which told me that she was not a Parisian. It was a pure French she spoke, and for a foreigner like myself a joy to listen to. She pronounced every word distinctly, using almost no slang, no colloquialisms. The words came out of her mouth fully formed and with a retarded tempo, as if she had rolled them on her palate before surrendering them to the void wherein the sound and the meaning are so swiftly transformed. Her laziness, which was voluptuous, feathered the words with a soft down; they came floating to my ears like balls of fluff. Her body was heavy, earth-laden, but the sounds which issued from her throat were like the clear notes of a bell.

She was made for it, as the saying goes, but she did not impress me as an out-and-out whore. That she would go with me, and take money for it, I knew—but that doesn't make a woman a whore.

She put a hand on me and, like a trained seal, my pecker rose jubilantly to her delicate caress.

"Contain yourself," she murmured, "it's bad to get excited too quickly."

"Let's get out of here," said I, beckoning the waiter.

"Yes," she said, "let's go somewhere where we can talk at leisure."

The less talking the better, I thought to

myself, as I gathered my things and escorted her to the street. A wonderful piece of ass, I reflected, watching her sail through the revolving door. I already saw her dangling on the end of my cock, a fresh, hefty piece of meat waiting to be cured and trimmed.

As we were crossing the boulevard she remarked how pleased she was to have found someone like me. She knew no one in Paris, she was lonesome. Perhaps I would take her around, show her the city? It would be amusing to be guided about the city, the capital of one's own country, by a stranger. Had I ever been to Amboise or Blois or Tours? Maybe we could take a trip together some day. *"Ça vous plairait?"*

We tripped along, chatting thus, until we came to a hotel which she seemed to know. "It's clean and cozy here," she said. "And if it's a little chilly, we will warm each other in bed." She squeezed my arm affectionately.

The room was as cozy as a nest. I waited a moment for soap and towels, tipped the maid, and locked the door. She had taken off her hat and fur piece, and stood waiting to embrace me at the window. What a warm, plantular piece of flesh! I thought she would burst into seed under my touch. In a few moments we started to undress. I sat down on the edge of the bed to unlace my shoes. She was standing beside me, pulling off her things. When I looked up she had nothing on but her stockings. She stood there, waiting for me to examine her more attentively. I got up and put my arms around her again, running my hands leisurely over the billowy folds of flesh. She pulled out of the embrace and, holding me at arm's length inquired coyly if I were not somewhat deceived.

"Deceived?" I echoed. "How do you mean?"

"Am I not too fat?" she said, dropping her eyes and resting them on her navel.

"Too fat? Why, you're marvelous. You're like a Renoir."

At this she blushed. "A Renoir?" she repeated, almost as if she had never heard the name. "No, you're joking."

"Oh, never mind. Come here, let me stroke that pussy of yours."

"Wait, I will first make my toilette." As

18

she moved towards the *bidet* she said: "You get into bed. Make it nice and toasty, yes?"

I undressed quickly, washed my cock out of politeness, and dove between the sheets. The *bidet* was right beside the bed. When she had finished her ablutions she began to dry herself with the thin, worn towel. I leaned over and grabbed her tousled bush, which was still a little dewy. She pushed me back into bed and, leaning over me, made a quick dive for it with her warm red mouth. I slipped a finger inside her to get the juice working. Then, pulling her on top of me, I sank it in up to the hilt. It was one of those cunts which fit like a glove. Her adroit muscular contractions soon had me gasping. All the while she licked my neck, my armpits, the lobes of my ears. With my two hands I lifted her up and down, rolling her pelvis round and round. Finally, with a groan, she bore down on me full weight; I rolled her over on her back, pulled her legs up over my shoulders, and went at her slam-bang. I thought I'd never stop coming; it came out in steady stream, as if from a garden hose. When I pulled away it seemed to me that I had an even bigger erection than when I plugged in.

"Ca c'est quelque chose," she said, putting her hand around my cock and fingering it appraisingly. "You know how to do it, don't you?"

We got up, washed, and crawled back into bed again. Reclining on an elbow, I ran my hand up and down her body. Her eyes were glowing as she lay back, thoroughly relaxed, her legs open, her flesh tingling. Nothing was said for several minutes. I lit a cigarette for her, put it in her mouth, and sank deep into the bed, staring contentedly at the ceiling.

"Are we going to see more of each other?" I asked after a time.

"That is up to you," she said, taking a deep puff. She turned over to put her cigarette out and then, drawing close, gazing at me steadily, smiling, but serious, she said in her low, warbling voice: "Listen, I must talk to you seriously. There is a great favor I wish to ask of you . . . I am in trouble, great trouble. Would you help me, if I asked you to?"

"Of course," I said, "but how?"

"I mean money," she said, quietly and simply. "I need a great deal . . . I *must* have it. I won't explain why. Just believe me, will you?"

I leaned over and yanked my pants off the chair. I fished out the bills and all the change that was in my pocket, and handed it to her.

"I'm giving you all I have," I said. "That's the best I can do."

She laid the money on the night table beside her without looking at it and, bending over, she kissed my brow. "You're a brick," she said. She remained bent over me, looking into my eyes with mute, strangled gratitude, then kissed me on the mouth, not passionately, but slowly, lingeringly, as if to convey the affection which she couldn't put into words and which she was too delicate to convey by offering her body.

"I can't say anything now," she said, falling back on the pillow. *"Je suis émue, c'est tout."* Then, after a brief pause, she added: "It's strange how one's own people are never as good to one as a stranger. You Americans are very kind, very gentle. We have much to learn from you."

It was such an old song to me, I almost felt ashamed of myself for having posed once again as the generous American. I explained to her that it was just an accident, my having so much money in my pocket. To this she replied that it was all the more wonderful, my gesture. "A Frenchman would hide it away," she said. "He would never give it to the first girl he met just because she was in need of help. He wouldn't believe her in the first place. *'Je connais la chanson,'* he would say."

I said nothing more. It was true and it wasn't true. It takes all sorts to make a world and, though up to that time I had never met a generous Frenchman, I believed that they existed. If I had told her how ungenerous my own friends had been, my countrymen, she would never have believed me. And if I had added that it was not generosity which had prompted me, but self-pity, myself giving to myself (because nobody could be as generous to me as I myself), she would probably have thought me slightly cracked.

I snuggled up to her and buried my head in her bosom. I slid my head down and licked her navel. Then farther down, kissing the thick clump of hair. She drew my head up slowly and, pulling me on top of her, buried her tongue in my mouth. My cock stiffened instantly; it slid into her just as naturally as an engine going into a switch. I had one of those long, lingering hard-ons which drive a woman mad. I jibbed her about at will, now over, now under her, then sidewise, then drawing it out slowly, tantalizingly, massaging the lips of the vulva with the bristling tip of my cock. Finally I pulled it out altogether and twirled it around her breasts. She looked at it in astonishment. "Did you come?" she asked. "No," I said. "We're going to try something else now," and I dragged her out of the bed and placed her in position for a proper, thorough back-scuttling. She reached up under her crotch and put it in for me, wiggling her ass around invitingly as she did so. Gripping her firmly around the waist, I shot it into her guts. "Oh, oh, that's marvelous, that's *wonderful*," she grunted, rolling her ass with a frenzied swing. I pulled it out again to give it an airing, rubbing it playfully against her buttocks. "No, no," she begged, "don't do that. Stick it in, stick it all the way in . . . I can't wait." Again she reached under and placed it for me, bending her back still more now, and pushing upward as if to trap the chandelier. I could feel it coming again, from the middle of my spine; I bent my knees slightly and pushed it in another notch or two. Then bango! it burst like a sky rocket.

It was well into the dinner hour when we parted down the street in front of a urinal. I hadn't made any definite appointment with her, nor had I inquired what her address might be. It was tacitly understood that the place to find her was at the café. Just as we were taking leave it suddenly occurred to me that I hadn't even asked her what her name was. I called her back and asked her—not for her full name but for her first name. "N-Y-S," she said, spelling it out. "Like the city, Nice." I walked off, saying it over and over to myself. I had never heard of a girl being called by that name before. It sounded like the name of a precious stone.

When I reached the Place Clichy I realized that I was ravenously hungry. I stood in front of a fish restaurant on the Avenue de Clichy, studying the menu which was posted outside. I felt like having clams, lobsters, oysters, snails, a broiled bluefish, a tomato omelette, some tender asparagus tips, a savory cheese, a loaf of bread, a bottle of chilled wine, some figs and nuts. I felt in my pocket, as I always do before entering a restaurant, and found a tiny sou. "Shit," I said to myself, "she might at least have spared me a few francs."

I set out at a quick pace to see if there was anything in the larder at home. It was a good half hour's walk to where we lived in Clichy, beyond the gates. Carl would already have had his dinner, but perhaps there would be a crust of bread and a little wine still standing on the table. I walked faster and faster, my hunger increasing with each step I took.

When I burst into the kitchen I saw at a

glance that he hadn't eaten. I searched everywhere but couldn't find a crumb. Nor were there any empty bottles about, which I could cash. I became frantic. I rushed out, determined to ask for credit at the little restaurant near the Place Clichy, where I often ate. Just outside the restaurant I lost my nerve and turned away. I now took to strolling about aimlessly, hoping that by some miracle I would bump into someone I knew. I knocked about for an hour or so, until I grew so exhausted that I decided to return home and go to bed. On the way I thought of a friend, a Russian, who lived near the outer boulevard. It was ages since I had seen him last. How could I walk in on him, like that, and ask for a hand-out? Then a brilliant thought hit me: I would go home, fetch the records, and hand them to him as a little gift. In that way it would be easier, after a few preliminaries, to suggest a sandwich or a piece of cake. I quickened my pace, though dog-tired and lame in the shanks.

When I got back to the house I saw that it was near midnight. That completely crushed me. It was useless to do any further foraging; I would go to bed and hope for something to turn up in the morning. As I was undressing I got another idea, this time not such a brilliant one, but still . . . I went to the sink and opened the little closet where the garbage can stood. I removed the cover and looked inside. There were a few bones and a hard crust of bread lying at the bottom. I fished out the dry crust, carefully scraped off the contaminated parts so as to waste as little as possible, and soaked it under the faucet. Then I bit into it slowly, extracting the utmost from each crumb. As I gulped it down a smile spread over my face, a broader and broader one. Tomorrow, I thought to myself, I shall go back to the shop and offer the books at half price, or a third, or a fourth. Ditto for the records. Ought to fetch ten francs, at least. Would have a good hearty breakfast, and then . . . Well, after that anything might happen. We'd see . . . I smiled some more, as if to a well-fed stomach. I was beginning to feel in excellent humor. That Nys, she must have had a corking meal. Probably with her lover. I hadn't the vaguest doubt but that she had a lover. Her great problem, her dilemma no doubt, had been how to feed him properly, how to buy him the clothes and other little things he craved. Well, it had been a royal fuck, even though I had fucked myself into the bargain. I could see her raising the napkin to her full ripe lips to wipe away the sauce from the tender chicken she had ordered. I wondered how her taste ran in wines. If we could only go to the Touraine country! But that would need a lot of jack. I'd never have that much money. Never. Just the same, no harm dreaming about it. I drank another glass of water. Putting the glass back, I espied a piece of Roquefort in a corner of the cupboard. If only there was just another crust of bread! To make sure I had overlooked nothing, I opened the garbage can again. A few bones lying in a scum of mildewed fat stared up at me.

I wanted another piece of bread, and I wanted it bad. Maybe I could borrow a hunk from a neighboring tenant. I opened the hall door and tiptoed out. There was a silence as of the grave. I put my ear to one of the doors and listened. A child coughed faintly. No use. Even if someone was awake it wasn't done. Not in France. Who ever heard of a Frenchman knocking at his neighbor's door in the dead of night to ask for a crust of bread? "Shit!" I muttered to myself, "to think of all the bread we've thrown into the garbage can!" I bit into the Roquefort grimly. It was old and sour; it crumbled to bits, like a piece of plaster that had been soaked in urine. That bitch, Nys! If only I knew her address I would go and beg a few francs of her. I must have been out of my mind not to hold out a little change. To give money to a whore is like throwing it down the sewer. Her great need! An extra chemise, most likely, or a pair of sheer silk hose glimpsed in passing a shop window.

I worked myself into a fine fury. All because there wasn't an extra crust of bread in the house. Idiotic! Thoroughly idiotic! In my delirium I began to dwell on malted milk shakes, and how, in America, there was always an extra glassful waiting for you in the shaker. That extra glassful was tantalizing. In America there was always *more* than you needed, not less. As I peeled my things off I felt my ribs. They stuck out like the sides of an accordion. That plump little bitch, Nys—she certainly was not dying of malnutrition. Once again, shit!— and to bed.

I had scarcely pulled the covers over me when I began laughing again. This time it was terrifying. I got to laughing so hysterically that I couldn't stop. It was like a thousand Roman candles going off at once. No matter what I thought of, and I tried to think of sad and even terrible things, the laughter continued. *Because of a little crust of bread!* That was the phrase which repeated itself intermittently, and which threw me into renewed fits of laughter.

I was only in bed about an hour when I heard Carl opening the door. He went straight to his room and closed his door. I was sorely tempted to ask him to go out and buy me a sandwich and a bottle of wine. Then I had a better idea. I would get up early, while he was still sound asleep and rifle his pockets. As I was tossing about, I heard him open the door of his room and go to the bathroom. He was giggling and whispering—to some floozy, most likely, whom he had picked up on the way home.

As he came out of the bathroom I called to him.

"So you're awake?" he said jubilantly. "What's the matter, are you sick?"

I explained that I was hungry, ravenously hungry. Had he any change on him?

"I'm cleaned out," he said. He said it cheerfully, as though it were nothing of importance.

"Haven't you got a franc at least?" I demanded.

"Don't worry about francs," he said, sitting on the edge of the bed with the air of a man who is about to confide a piece of important news. "We've got bigger things to worry about now. I brought a girl home with me—a waif. She can't be more than fourteen. I just gave her a lay. Did you hear me? I hope I didn't knock her up. She's a virgin."

"You mean she *was*," I put in.

"Listen, Joey," he said, lowering his voice to make it sound more convincing, "we've got to do something for her. She has no place to stay . . . she ran away from home. I found her walking about in a trance, half-starved, and a little demented, I thought at first. Don't worry, she's O.K. Not very bright, but a good sort. Probably from a good family. She's just a child . . . you'll see. Maybe I'll marry her when she comes of age. Anyway there's no money. I spent my last cent buying her a meal. Too bad you had to go without dinner. You should have been with *us*. We had oysters, lobster, shrimps—and a wonderful wine. A Chablis, year . . ."

"Fuck the year!" I shouted. "Don't tell me about what you ate. I'm as empty as an ash can. Now we've got three mouths to feed and no money, not a sou."

"Take it easy, Joey," he said smilingly, "you know I always keep a few francs in my pocket for an emergency." He dove into his pocket and pulled out the change. It amounted to three francs sixty altogether. "That'll get you a breakfast," he said. "To-morrow's another day."

At that moment the girl stuck her head through the doorway. Carl jumped up and brought her to the bed. "Colette," he said, as I put out my hand to greet her. "What do you think of her?"

Before I had time to answer, the girl turned to him and, almost as if frightened, asked what language we were speaking.

"Don't you know English when you hear it?" said Carl, giving me a glance which said I told you she wasn't very bright.

Blushing with confusion, the girl explained quickly that it sounded at first like German, or perhaps Belgian.

"There is no Belgian!" snorted Carl. Then to me: "She's a little idiot. But look at those breasts! Pretty ripe for fourteen, what? She swears she's seventeen, but I don't believe her."

Colette stood there listening to the strange language, unable even yet to grasp the fact that Carl could speak anything but French. Finally she demanded to know if he really was French. It seemed quite important to her.

"Sure I'm French," said Carl blithely. "Can't you tell by my speech? Do I talk like a *Boche?* Want to see my passport?"

"Better not show her that," I said, remembering that he carried a Czech passport.

"Would you like to come in and look at the sheets?" he said, putting an arm around Colette's waist. "We'll have to throw them away, I guess. I can't take them to the laundry; they'd suspect me of having committed a crime."

"Get *her* to wash them," I said jocularly. "There's a lot she can do around here if she wants to keep house for us."

"So you do want her to stay? You know it's illegal, don't you? We can go to jail for this."

"Better get her a pair of pajamas, or a nightgown," I said, "because if she's going to walk around at night in that crazy shift of yours I may forget myself and rape her."

He looked at Colette and burst out laughing.

"What is it?" she exclaimed. "Are you making fun of me? Why doesn't your friend talk French?"

"You're right," I said. "From now on we're talking French and nothing but French. *D'accord?*"

A childish grin spread over her face. She bent down and gave me a kiss on both cheeks. As she did so her boobies fell out and brushed my face. The little shift fell open all the way down, revealing an exquisitely full young body.

"Jesus, take her away and keep her locked up in your room," I said. "I won't be responsible for what happens if she's going to prowl around in that get-up while you're out."

Carl packed her off to his room and sat down again on the edge of the bed. "We've got a problem on our hands, Joey," he began, "and you've got to help me. I don't care what you do with her when my back is turned. I'm not jealous, you know that. But you mustn't let her fall into the hands of the police. If they catch her they'll send her away—and they'll probably send us away too. The thing is, what to tell the concierge? I can't lock her up like a dog. Maybe I'll say she's a cousin of mine, here on a visit. Nights, when I go to work, take her to the movies. Or take her for a walk. She's easy to please. Teach her geography or something—she doesn't know a thing. It'll be good for you, Joey. You'll improve your French . . . And don't knock her up, if you can help it. I can't think about money for abortions now. Besides, I don't know anymore where my Hungarian doctor lives."

I listened to him in silence. Carl had a genius for getting involved in difficult situations. The trouble was, or perhaps it was a virtue, that he was incapable of saying No. Most people say No immediately, out of a blind preservative instinct. Carl alway said Yes, Sure, Certainly. He would compromise himself for life on the impulse of a moment, knowing deep down, I suppose, that the same preservative instinct which made others say No would become operative at the crucial moment. With all his warm, generous impulses, his instinctive kindliness and tenderness, he was also the most elusive fellow I have ever known. Nobody, no power on earth could pin him down, once he made up his mind to free himself. He was as slippery as an eel, cunning, ingenious, absolutely reckless. He flirted with danger, not out of courage, but because it gave him an opportunity to sharpen his wits, to practice jujitsu. When drunk he became imprudent and audacious. On a dare he would walk into a police station and shout *Merde!* at the top of his lungs. If he were apprehended he would apologize, saying that he must have been temporarily out of his mind. And he would get away with it! Usually he did these little tricks so fast that, before the astonished guardians of the peace could come to their senses, he would be a block or two away, perhaps sitting on a terrace, sipping a beer and looking as innocent as a lamb.

In a pinch Carl always hocked his type-writer. In the beginning he could get as much as four hundred francs on it, which was no mean sum then. He took extremely good care of his machine because he was frequently obliged to borrow on it. I retain a most vivid image of him dusting and oiling the thing each time he sat down to write, and of carefully putting the cover over it when he had finished writing. I noticed too that he was secretly relieved whenever he put it in hock: it meant that he could declare a holiday without having a guilty conscience. But when he had spent the money, and had only time on his hands, he would become irritable; it was at such times, he swore, that he always got his most brilliant ideas. If the ideas became really burning and obsessive, he would buy himself a little notebook and go off somewhere to write it out in longhand, using the most handsome Parker pen I have ever seen. He would never admit to me that he was making notes on the sly, not until long afterwards. No, he would come home looking sour and disgruntled, saying that he had been obliged to piss the day away. If I suggested that he go to the newspaper office, where he worked nights, and use one of their machines, he would invent a good reason why such a procedure was impossible.

I mention this business of the machine and his never having it when he needed it, because it was one of his ways of making things difficult for himself. It was an artistic device which, despite all evidences to the contrary, always worked out advantageously for him. If he had not been deprived of the machine at periodic intervals he would have run dry and, through sheer despondency, remained barren far beyond the normal curve. His ability to remain under water, so to speak, was extraordinary. Most people, observing him under these submerged conditions, usually gave him up as lost. But he was never really in danger of going under for good; if he gave that illusion it was only because he had a more than usual need of sympathy and attention. When he emerged, and began narrating his under-water experiences, it was like a revelation. It proved, for one thing, that he had been very much alive all the while. And not only alive, but extremely observant. As if he had swum about like a fish in a bowl; as if he had seen everything through a magnifying glass.

A strange bird he was, in many ways. One who could, moreover, take his own feelings apart, like the workings of a Swiss watch, and examine them.

For an artist bad situations are just as fertile as good ones, sometimes even more so. For him all experience is fruitful and capable of being converted to credit. Carl was the type of artist who fears to use up his credit. Instead of expanding the realm of experience, he preferred to safeguard his credit. This he did by reducing his natural flow to a thin trickle.

Life is constantly providing us with new funds, new resources, even when we are reduced to immobility. In life's ledger there is no such thing as frozen assets.

What I am getting at is that Carl, unknown to himself, was cheating himself. He was always endeavoring to hold back instead of giving forth. Thus, when he did break out, whether in life or with the pen, his adventures took on an hallucinating quality. The very things he feared to experience, or to express, were the things which, at the wrong moment, that is to say when least prepared, he was forced to deal with. His audacity, consequently, was bred of desperation. He behaved sometimes like a cornered rat, even in his work. People would wonder whence he derived the courage, or the inventiveness, to do or say certain things. They forgot that he was ever at a point beyond which the ordinary man commits suicide. For Carl suicide offered no solution. If he could die and write about his death, that would be fine. He used to say on occasion that he couldn't imagine himself ever dying, barring some universal calamity. He said it not in the spirit of a man filled with a superabundance of vitality; he said it as one who refused to waste his energy, who had never allowed the clock to run down.

When I think about this period, when we lived together in Clichy, it seems like a stretch in Paradise. There was only one real problem, and that was food. All other ills were imaginary. I used to tell him so now and then, when he complained about being a slave. He used to say I was an incurable optimist, but it wasn't optimism, it was the deep realization that, even though the world was busy digging its grave, there was still time to enjoy life, to be merry, carefree, to work or not to work.

It lasted a good year, this period, and during this time I wrote *Black Spring*, rode the bike up and down the Seine, made trips to the Midi and to the Châteaux country, and finally went on a mad picnic with Carl to Luxembourg.

It was a period when cunt was in the air. The English girls were at the Casino de Paris; they ate at a *prix fixe* restaurant near the Place Blanche. We became friends with the whole troupe, pairing off finally with a gorgeously beautiful Scotch girl and her friend from Ceylon who was a Eurasian. The Scotch girl eventually handed Carl a beautiful dose of clap which she contracted from her Negro lover at Melody's Bar. But that's getting ahead of my story. There was also the hat check girl from a little dance place on the Rue Fontaine, where we used to drop in on Carl's night off. She was a nymphomaniac, very gay, very modest in her demands. She introduced us to a flock of girls who hung about the bar and who, when they could get nothing better than us, would take us on for a song at the end of an evening. One of them always insisted on taking us both home with her—she said it excited her. Then there was the girl, at the *épicerie,* whose American husband had deserted her; she liked to be taken to the movies and then to bed, where she would lie awake all night talking broken English. It didn't matter to her which of us she slept with, because we both spoke English. And finally there was

Jeanne, who had been jilted by my friend Fillmore. Jeanne would drop in at odd hours of the day or night, always loaded with bottles of white wine, which she drank like a fish to console herself. She would do everything but go to bed with us. She was an hysterical type, alternating between moods of extreme gayety and blackest melancholy. In her cups she became lascivious and boisterous. You could undress her, stroke her twat, maul her teats, even suck her off, if you wanted to, but the moment you got your prick near her cunt she flew off the handle. One minute she would bite you passionately and pull at your cock with her strong peasant hands, the next minute she would be weeping violently and shoving you away with her feet or striking out blindly with her fists. Usually the place was a wreck when she left. Sometimes, in her precipitate rages, she would run out of the house half naked, to return almost immediately, coy as a kitten and full of apologies. At such moments, if one wanted to, one might have given her a good fuck, but we never did. "You take her," I can hear Carl say, "I've had enough of that bitch, she's mad." I felt the same way about her. Out of friendship I'd give her a dry fuck against the radiator, fill her up with cognac, and pack her off. She seemed extraordinarily grateful, at such moments, for these little attentions. Just like a child.

There was another, whom we met later through Jeanne, an innocent-looking creature but dangerous as a viper. She dressed in bizarre fashion, ludicrously, I might add, due to her Pocahontas fixation. She was a Parisian and the mistress of a famous Surrealist poet, a fact we were ignorant of at the time.

Shortly after we had made her acquaintance we met her one night walking by herself along the fortifications. It was a strange thing to be doing at that hour of the night, and not a little suspect. She returned our greeting as if in a trance. She seemed to remember our faces but had obviously forgotten where or when we had met. Nor did she seem to be interested in refreshing her memory. She accepted our company as she would have accepted the company of anyone who happened along. She made no

44

attempt at conversation; her talk was more
like a monologue which we had interrupted. Carl, who was adept at such things,
fed her along in his own schizophrenic way.
Gradually we steered her back to the house
and up to our rooms—as if she were a sleep-
walker. Never a question from her as to
where we were going, what we were doing.
She walked in and sat down on the divan
as if she were at home. She asked for
some tea and a sandwich, in the same tone
of voice that she might have used in addressing the *garçon* at a café. And in the
same tone of voice she asked us how much
we would give her for staying with us. In
her matter-of-fact way she added that she
needed two hundred francs for her rent,
which was due next day. Two hundred
francs was probably a good deal, she remarked, but that was the sum she needed.
She spoke like one reflecting on the condition of the larder. "Now let me see, we
need eggs, butter, some bread and perhaps
a little jam." Just like that. "If you want
me to suck you off, or if you want to do it
dog-fashion, whatever you like, it's all the

same to me," she said, sipping her tea like a duchess at a charity bazaar. "My breasts are still firm and enticing," she continued, undoing her blouse and extracting a handful. "I know men who would pay a thousand francs to sleep with me, but I can't be bothered hunting them up. I must have two hundred francs, no more, no less." She paused a minute to glance at a book on the table at her elbow, then continued in the same toneless voice: "I have some poems, too, which I will show you later. They may be better than those," referring to the volume she had just glanced at.

At this juncture Carl, who was standing in the doorway, began signaling me in deaf and dumb fashion, to let me know she was crazy. The girl, who had been rummaging in her bag to extract her poems, suddenly looked up and, catching the embarrassed look on Carl's face, remarked calmly and soberly that he was out of his mind. "Is there a *bidet* in the bathroom?" she asked in the same breath. "I have one poem which I will read to you in a moment; it is about a dream I had the other night." So saying, she stood up and slowly took off her blouse and skirt. "Tell your friend to get himself ready," she said, undoing her hair. "I will sleep with him first."

At this Carl gave a start. He was getting more and more frightened of her, and at the same time he was convulsed with suppressed laughter.

"Wait a minute," he said, "have a little wine before you wash. It will do you good." He quickly brought out a bottle and poured her a glass. She quaffed it as if she were quenching her thirst with a glass of water. "Take off my shoes and stockings," she said, leaning back against the wall and holding out her glass for more. "*Ce vin est une saloperie*," she added in her monotonous tone, "but I am used to it. You have the two hundred francs, I suppose? I must have exactly that amount. Not one hundred and seventy-five or one hundred and eighty. Give me your hand . . ." She took Carl's hand, which had been fumbling with her garter, and placed it on her quim. "There are fools who have offered as much as five thousand francs to touch that. Men are stupid. I let you touch it for nothing. Here, give me another glassful. It tastes less vile when you drink a lot of it. *What time is it?*"

As soon as she had closeted herself in the bathroom Carl let loose. He laughed like a madman. Frightened, that's what he was. "I'm not going to do it," he said. "She might bite my prick off. Let's get her out of here. I'll give her fifty francs and put her in a taxi."

"I don't think she'll let you do that," said I, enjoying his discomfiture. "She means business. Besides, if she's really goofy she may forget all about the money."

"That's an idea, Joey," he exclaimed enthusiastically. "I never thought of that. You have a criminal mind. But listen, don't leave me in there alone with her, will you? You can watch us—she doesn't give a damn. She'd fuck a dog, if we asked her to. She's a somnambulist."

I got into my pajamas and tucked myself in bed. She remained a long time in the bathroom. We were beginning to worry.

"Better go and see what's up," I said.

"You go," he said. "I'm afraid of her."

I got up and knocked at the bathroom door.

"Come in," she said, in the same dull, toneless voice.

I opened the door and found her stark naked, her back turned to me. With her lip rouge she was writing a poem on the wall.

I went back to summon Carl. "She must be out of her mind," I said. "She's smearing the walls with her poems."

While Carl was reading her verse aloud I got a really clever idea. She wanted two hundred francs. *Good*. I had no money on me, but I suspected that Carl had—he had only been paid the day before. I knew if I looked in the volume marked *Faust,* in his room, I would find two or three hundred-franc bills flattened between the leaves. Carl was ignorant of the fact that I had discovered his secret vault. I had come upon it by accident one day when searching for a dictionary. I knew that he continued to keep a little sum hidden away in this volume of *Faust,* because I went back several times later to verify the fact. I let him starve with me for almost two days once, knowing all the time that the money was there. I was extremely curious to see how long he could hold out on me.

My mind now began working rapidly. I would navigate the two of them into *my* room, extract the money from the vault, hand it to her, and, upon her next trip to the bathroom, I would take the money out her bag and put it back in Goethe's *Faust*. I would let Carl give her the fifty francs he had been talking about; that would pay for the taxi. She wouldn't look for the two hundred francs until the morning; if she were really crazy she wouldn't miss the money, and if she weren't crazy she would probably tell herself she had lost the money in the taxi. In any case she would leave the house as she had entered it—in a trance. She would never stop to note the address on her way out, that I felt certain of.

The plan worked out admirably, except that we had to give her a fuck before bundling her off. It all happened quite un-expectedly. I had given her the two hun-dred francs, to Carl's amazement, and I had persuaded him to fork out the fifty francs for a taxi. She was busy the while writing another poem, in pencil, on a scrap of paper which she had torn from a book. I was sitting on the divan and she was standing in front of me stark naked, her ass staring me in the face. I thought I would see if she'd continue writing should I put a finger up her crack. I did it very gently, as if exploring the delicate petals of a rose. She kept on scribbling, without the least murmur of approval or disapproval, merely opening her legs a little more for my convenience. In an instant I had a tremendous erection. I got up and shoved my prick inside her. She sprawled forward over the desk, the pencil still in her hand. "Bring her over here," said Carl, who was in bed and squirming about like an eel now. I turned her around, got it in frontwise and, lifting her off her feet, I dragged her over to the bed. Carl pounced on her immediately, grunting like a wild boar. I let him have his fill, and then I let her have it again, from the rear. When it was over she asked for some wine, and while I was filling the glass she began to laugh. It was a weird laugh, like nothing I had ever heard before. Suddenly she stopped, asked for paper and

pencil, then a pad with which to support
the paper. She sat up, put her feet over the
edge of the bed, and began composing
another poem. When she had written two
or three lines she asked for her revolver.

"*Revolver?*" shrieked Carl, springing out
of bed like a rabbit. "*What revolver?*"

"The one in my bag," she calmly replied.
"I feel like shooting someone now. You
have had a good time for your two hundred
francs—now it is my turn." With this she
made a leap for the bag. We pounced on
her and threw her to the floor. She bit and
scratched and kicked with all her strength.

"See if there's a gun in the bag," said
Carl, pinning her down. I jumped up,
grabbed the bag, and saw that there was
no gun in it; at the same time I extracted
the two bills and hid them under the paper
weight on the desk.

"Throw some water on her, *quick*," said
Carl. "I think she's going to have a fit."

I rushed to the sink, filled a pitcher full
of water and threw it over her. She gasped,
wiggled a bit, like a fish out of water, sat
up, and with a weird smile, said: "*Ça y est,
c'est bien assez . . . laissez-moi sortir.*"

Good, I thought to myself, at last we're rid of her. To Carl: "Watch her close, I'll get her things. We'll have to dress her and put her in a cab."

We dried her off and dressed her as best we could. I had an uneasy feeling that she would start something again, before we could get her out of the place. And what if she should start yelling in the street, just for the devil of it?

We dressed in turn, rapidly, watching her like a hawk. Just as we were ready to go she thought of the scrap of paper she had left on the desk—the unfinished poem. In groping about for it her eyes fell on the bills tucked under the paper weight.

"My money!" she yelled.

"Don't be silly," I said calmly, holding her by the arm. "You don't think we would rob you, do you? You've got your money in your bag."

She gave me a quick, penetrating glance and dropped her eyes. "*Je vous demande pardon,*" she said. "*Je suis très nerveuse ce soir.*"

"You said it," said Carl, hustling her to the door. "That was clever of you, Joey," he said in English, as we went down the stairs.

"Where do you live?" asked Carl, when we had hailed a taxi.

"Nowhere," she replied. "I'm tired. Tell him to drop me off at a hotel, any hotel."

Carl seemed touched. "Do you want us to go along with you?" he asked.

"No," she said. "I want to sleep."

"Come on," I said, pulling him away. "She'll be all right."

I slammed the door and waved good night. Carl stood looking at the receding taxi in a dazed way.

"What's the matter with you? You're not worried about her, are you? If she's crazy she won't need money, nor a hotel either."

"I know, but just the same . . . Listen, Joey, you're a hard-hearted son of a bitch. *And the money!* Jesus, we fucked her good and proper."

"Yes," I said, "it was lucky I knew where you kept your dough."

"You mean that was *my* money?" he said, suddenly realizing what I meant.

"Yes, Joey, the eternal feminine always draws us on. A great poem, *Faust*."

At this he went over to the wall, leaned against it, then doubled over with hysterical laughter. "I thought I was the quick-witted one," he said, "but I'm only a novice. Listen, tomorrow we'll spend that money. We'll have a good feed somewhere. I'll take you to a real restaurant for a change."

"By the way," I remarked, "was her poetry any good? I didn't have a chance to study it. I mean those verses in the bathroom."

"There was one good line," he said. "The rest was lunatical."

"Lunatical? There's no such word in English."

"Well, that's what it was. Crazy wouldn't describe it. You have to coin a new word for it. *Lunatical.* I like that word. I'm going to use it . . . And now I'm going to tell *you* something, Joey. You remember the revolver?"

"What revolver? There *was* no revolver."

"Yes, there was," he replied, giving me a queer smile. "I hid it in the bread box."

"So you went through her bag first, is that it?"

"I was just looking for a little change," he said, hanging his head, as though he felt sheepish about it.

"I don't believe that," I said. "There must have been some other reason."

"You're pretty bright, Joey," he retorted gaily, "but you miss a thing or two now and then. Do you remember when she squatted down to make pee pee—up at the ramparts? She had given me her bag to hold. I felt something hard inside, something like a gun. I didn't say anything because I didn't want to frighten you. But when you started walking her back to the house I got scared. When she went to the bathroom I opened the bag and found the gun. It was loaded. Here are the bullets, if you don't believe me . . ."

I looked at them in complete stupefaction. A cold chill ran up and down my spine.

"She must have been really crazy," I said, heaving a sigh of relief.

"No," said Carl, "she's not crazy at all. She's playing at it. And her poems aren't crazy either—they're lunatical. She may have been hypnotized. Somebody may have put her to sleep, put the gun in her hand, and told her to bring back two hundred francs."

"That's really crazy!" I exclaimed.

He made no answer. He walked along with head down, silent for a few minutes. "What puzzles me," he said, looking up, "is this—why did she forget about the revolver so quickly? And why didn't she look in her bag for the money when you lied to her? I think she knew that the revolver was gone, and the money too. I think she was frightened of us. And now I'm getting frightened again myself. I think we'd better take a hotel for the night. Tomorrow you take a little trip somewhere . . . stay away a few days."

We turned without another word and started walking rapidly towards Montmartre. We were panic-stricken . . .

This little incident precipitated our flight to Luxembourg. But I am months ahead of my story. Let me go back to our *ménage à trois*.

Colette, the homeless waif, soon became

a combination of Cinderella, concubine and cook. We had to teach her everything, including the art of brushing her teeth. She was at the awkward age, always dropping things, stumbling, getting lost, and so on. Now and then she would disappear for a couple of days at a stretch. What she did in these intervals it was impossible to discover. The more we questioned her the more torpid and blank she became. Sometimes she would go out for a walk in the morning and return at midnight with a stray cat or a pup she had found in the street. Once we followed her for a whole afternoon, just to see how she passed the time. It was like following a sleep-walker. All she did was to ramble from one street to another, aimlessly, listlessly, stopping to peer through shop windows, rest on a bench, feed the birds, buy herself a lollypop, stand for minutes on end as if in a trance, then striking out again in the same aimless, listless fashion. We followed her for five hours to discover nothing than that we had a child on our hands.

Carl was touched by her simple-mindedness. He was also getting worn out from the heavy sexual diet. And a little irritated because she was eating up all his spare time. He had given up all thought of writing, first because the machine was in hock, and second because he no longer had a minute to himself. Colette, poor soul, had absolutely no idea what to do with herself. She could lie in bed the whole afternoon, fucking her brains out, and be ready for more when Carl arrived from work. Carl usually came home about three in the morning. Often he would not get out of bed until seven in the evening, just in time to eat and rush to work. After a siege of it he would beg me to take a stab at her. "I'm fucked dry," he would say. "The half-wit, she's got all her brains in her cunt."

But Colette had no attraction for me. I was in love with Nys, who was still hanging out at the Café Wepler. We had become good friends. No question of money any more. True, I would bring her little gifts, but that was different somehow. Now and then I would induce her to take the afternoon off. We would go to little places along the Seine, or take a train to some nearby forest, where we would lie in the grass and fuck to our heart's content. I never pumped her about her past. It was always about the future that we talked. At least *she* did. Like so many French women, her dream was to find a little house in the country, somewhere in the Midi, preferably. She didn't care much for Paris. It was unhealthy, she would say.

"And what would you do with yourself to pass the time away?" I once asked.

"What would I *do?*" she repeated in astonishment. "I would do nothing. I would just live."

What an idea! What a sane idea! I envied her her phlegm, her indolence, her insouciance. I would urge her to talk about it at length, about doing nothing, I mean. It was an ideal I had never flirted with. To accomplish it one must have an empty mind, or else a full rich one. It would be better, I used to think, to have an empty mind.

Just to watch Nys eat was inspiring. She enjoyed every morsel of her food, which she selected with great care. By care I don't mean concern about calories and vitamins. No, she was careful to choose the things she liked, and which agreed with her, because she relished them. She could drag the meal out interminably, her good humor constantly augmenting, her indolence becoming more and more seductive, her spirit growing keener, livelier, brighter. A good meal, a good talk, a good fuck—what better way to pass the day? There were no worms devouring her conscience, no cares which she couldn't throw off. Floating with the tide, nothing more. She would produce no children, contribute nothing to the welfare of the community, leave no mark upon the world in going. But wherever she went she would make life easier, more attractive, more fragrant. And that is no little thing. Every time I left her I had the feeling of a day well spent. I wished that I too could take life in that same easy, natural way. Sometimes I wished I were a female, like her, possessing nothing more than an attractive cunt. How wonderful to put one's cunt to work and use one's brains for pleasure! To fall in love with happiness! To become as useless as possible! To develop a conscience tough as a crocodile's skin! And when old and no longer attrac-

tive, to buy a fuck, if needs be. Or buy a
dog and train him to do what's what. Die,
when the time came, naked and alone,
without guilt, without regret, without remorse . . .

That's how I would dream after spending a day with Nys in the open.

What a pleasure it would be to steal a
fat sum and hand it to her just as she was
taking off. Or accompany her part of the
way, as far as Orange, say, or Avignon.
Piss away a month or two, like a vagrant,
basking in her warm indolence. Wait on
her hand and foot, just to enjoy her enjoyment.

Nights when I couldn't see her—when
she was taken—I would wander around by
myself, stopping off at little bars in the
side streets, or at subterranean dives, where
other girls plied their trade in stupid, sense-
less fashion. Sometimes, out of sheer boredom, I would take one on, even though it
left the taste of ashes.

Often, on returning to the house, Colette
would still be up and prowling about in
that ridiculous Japanese shift which Carl
had picked up at a bazaar. Somehow we

never seemed able to raise the money to buy her a pair of pajamas. Usually I found her just about to have a little bite. Trying to keep awake, poor kid, in order to greet Carl upon his return from work. I would sit down and have a bite with her. We would talk, in desultory fashion. She never had anything to say worth listening to. She had no aspirations, no dreams, no desires. She was as cheerful as a cow, obedient as a slave, attractive as a doll. She was not stupid, she was dumb. Dumb the way a beast is. Nys, on the other hand, was not unintelligent. Lazy, yes. Lazy as sin. Everything Nys spoke about was interesting, even when it was about nothing. A gift which I prize far above the ability to talk intelligently. In fact, such talk seems to me to be of the first order. It contributes to life, whereas the other, the cultivated jargon, saps one's strength, makes everything sterile, futile, meaningless. But Colette, as I say, had only the dull-wittedness of a heifer. When you touched her you felt a cool, uninspired flesh, like jello. You could caress her buttocks as she poured your coffee, but it was like fondling a door-knob.

Her modesty was more that of an animal than of a human being. She held her hand over her cunt as if to conceal something ugly, not something dangerous. She would hide her cunt and leave her boobies exposed. If she came to the bathroom and found me taking a leak, she would stand in the doorway and converse with me in a matter of fact way. It didn't excite her to see a man urinating; she got excited only when you got on top of her and pissed inside her.

One night, arriving home rather late, I found I had forgotten my key. I knocked loudly but there was no answer. I thought perhaps she had gone off again on one of her innocent peregrinations. There was nothing to do but walk slowly towards Montmartre and catch Carl on his way home from work. About half-way to the Place Clichy I ran into him; I told him that Colette had probably flown the coop. Back at the house we found the lights on full blast. Colette was not there however, nor had she taken any of her belongings. It looked as though she had simply gone for a walk. That very morning Carl had been saying that he would marry her as soon as she came of age. I had a good laugh at their antics, she hanging out the bedroom window and he out the kitchen window, bellowing so that all the neighbors could hear: *"Bonjour, Madame Oursel, comment ça va ce matin?"*

Now he was depressed. He was certain the police had come and taken her away. "They'll be calling for *me* soon," he said. "This is the end."

We decided to go out, make a night of it. It was a little after three in the morning. The Place Clichy was dead except for a few bars which stayed open all night. The whore with the wooden leg was still at her post opposite the Gaumont Palace; she had her own faithful little clientele which kept her busy. We had a bite near the Place Pigalle, amid a group of early morning vultures. We looked in at the little dance place where our friend, the hat check girl, was posted, but they were just closing the joint. We zigzagged up the hill towards the Sacré Cœur. At the foot of the cathedral we rested a while, gazing out over the sea of twinkling lights. At night Paris becomes magnified. The illumination, softer from above, lessens the cruelty and sordidness of the streets. At night, from Montmartre, Paris is truly magical; it lies in the hollow of a bowl like an enormous splintered gem.

With the dawn Montmartre becomes indescribably lovely. A pink flush suffuses the mild-white walls. The huge advertisements, painted in brilliant reds and blues on the pale walls, stand out with a freshness which is nothing short of voluptuous. Coming around the side of the hill we ran into a group of young nuns looking so pure and virginal, so thoroughly rested, so calm and dignified, that we felt ashamed of ourselves. A little farther along we stumbled on a flock of goats picking their way erratically down the precipitous slope; behind them a full-blown cretin followed leisurely, blowing a few strange notes now and then. The atmosphere was one of utter tranquillity, utter peace; it might have been a morning of the fourteenth century.

We slept until almost evening that day. Still no sign of Colette, still no visit from the police. The next morning, however, towards noon, there was an ominous knock at the door. I was in my room, typing. Carl answered the door. I heard Colette's voice, and then the voice of a man. Presently I heard a woman's voice also. I continued typing. I wrote whatever came into my head, just to maintain the pretense of being occupied.

Presently Carl appeared, looking harried and distraught. "Did she leave her watch here?" he asked. "They're looking for the watch."

"Who are *they?*" I asked.

"Her mother is here . . . I don't know who the man is. A detective, maybe. Come in a minute, I'll introduce you."

The mother was a beautiful-looking creature of middle age, well groomed, almost distinguished-looking. The man, who was soberly and sedately dressed, looked like a barrister. Everyone spoke in low tones, as if a death had just occurred.

I sensed immediately that my presence was not without effect.

"Are you also a writer?" It was the man who spoke.

I answered politely that I was.

"Do you write in French?" he asked.

To this I made a very tactful, flattering reply, bemoaning the fact that, although I had been in France some five or six years and was conversant with French literature, even translating now and then, my native inadequacies had prevented me from mastering his beautiful language sufficiently to express myself as I wished.

I had summoned all my resources to phrase this flubdub eloquently and correctly. It seemed to me that it went straight to the target.

As for the mother, she was studying the titles of the books which were piled on Carl's work table. Impulsively she singled one out and handed it to the man. It was the last volume of Proust's celebrated work. The man turned from the book to survey Carl with new eyes. There was a fleeting, grudging deference in his expression. Carl, somewhat embarrassed, explained that he was at work on an essay intended to show the relation between Proust's metaphysic and the occult tradition, particularly the doctrine of Hermes Trismegistus, whom he was enamored of.

"*Tiens, tiens,*" said the man, raising an eyebrow significantly, and fixing us both with a severe yet not wholly condemnatory gaze. "Would you be so kind as to leave us alone with your friend for a few minutes?" he said, turning to me.

"Most certainly," I said, and went back to my room, where I resumed my hit or miss typing.

They were closeted in Carl's room for a good half-hour, it seemed to me. I had written some eight or ten pages of sheer babble, which not even the wildest Surrealist could make head or tail of, by the time they came to my room to say goodbye. I bade farewell to Colette as if she were a little orphan whom we had rescued and whom we were now returning safely to her long-lost parents. I inquired if they had found the watch. They had not, but they hoped that *we* would. It was a little keepsake, they explained.

As soon as the door had closed on them, Carl rushed into the room and put his arms around me. "Joey, I think you saved my life. Or maybe it was Proust. That sour-faced bastard was certainly impressed.

Literature! So French, that. Even the police are literary-minded here. And your
being an American—a famous writer, I
said—that raised our stock enormously.
You know what he told me when you left
the room? That he was Colette's legal
guardian. She's fifteen, by the way, but
she's run away from home before. Anyway, he said it would be a ten year sentence, if he were to bring me to court. He
asked me did I know that. I said yes. I
guess he was surprised that I made no attempt to defend myself. But what surprised
him more was to find out that we were
writers. The French have a great respect
for writers, you know that. A writer is
never an ordinary criminal. He had expected to find a couple of Apaches, I guess.
Or blackmailers. When he saw you he
weakened. He asked me afterwards what
kind of books you wrote, and if any of
them had been translated. I told him you
were a philosopher, and that you were
rather difficult to translate . . ."

"That was a fantastic line you gave him
about Hermes Trismegistus," I said. "How
did you happen to think that up?"

70

"I didn't," said Carl. "I was so damned scared, I said whatever came into my head . . . By the way, another thing that impressed him was *Faust*—because it was in German. There were some English books too—Lawrence, Blake, Shakespeare. I could almost hear him saying to himself, 'These fellows can't be so very bad. The child might have fallen into worse hands.' "

"But what did the mother have to say?"

"The *mother!* Did you have a good look at her? She was not only beautiful, she was divine. Joey, the moment I set eyes on her I fell in love with her. She hardly said a word the whole time. At the end she said to me: 'Monsieur, we will not press the case against you, on condition that you promise us never to attempt to see Colette again. Is that understood?' I hardly heard what she said, I was so confused. I blushed and stammered like a boy. If she had said, 'Monsieur, you will please come with us to the police station,' I would have said, '*Oui, Madame, à vos ordres.*' I was going to kiss her hand, but then I thought that might be going too far. Did you notice the perfume she used? That was . . ." He reeled

off some *marque* with a number, as if I
should be impressed. "You don't know
anything about perfumes, I forgot. Listen,
only women of breeding use perfumes like
that. She could have been a duchess or a
marquise. Too bad it wasn't the mother I
picked up. By the way, this will make a
good ending for my book, what?"

A very good ending, I thought to myself.
As a matter of fact, he did write the story
some months later, and it was one of the
best things he ever did, especially the pas-
sage about Proust and *Faust*. All the time
he was writing it he raved about the
mother. He seemed to have forgotten about
Colette completely.

Well, this episode was hardly over when
the English girls appeared on the scene,
and then the grocery girl who was crazy to
learn English, and then Jeanne, and between times the hat check girl, and now
and then a tart from the impasse just behind the Café Wepler—from the trap, as
we called it, because to get by that little
alley at night on the way home was like
running the gauntlet.

And then came the somnambulist with

the revolver, which had us on tenterhooks for a few days.

Early one morning, after we had sat up all night polishing off some Algerian wine, Carl broached the idea of taking a hurried vacation for a few days. There was a large map of Europe hanging on my wall which we examined feverishly to see how far we might go with the limited funds at our disposal. We thought at first of going to Brussels, but on second thoughts we abandoned the idea. The Belgians were uninteresting, we agreed. For about the same fare we could go to Luxembourg. We were quite drunk, and Luxembourg seemed like just the right place to go to at six o'clock in the morning. We didn't pack any valises; all we needed were our tooth-brushes, which we forgot in the scramble to catch the train.

A few hours later we crossed the border and stepped into the lacquered, upholstered train which was to take us to the *opéra bouffe* country which I for one was very eager to see. We arrived towards noon, sleepy and dazed. We had a heavy lunch, washed down with the wine of the country, and tumbled into bed. About six o'clock we roused ourselves and ambled outdoors. It was a peaceful, fat, easy-going land, with sounds of German music everywhere; the faces of the inhabitants were stamped with a sort of cow-like bliss.

It was no time before we had made friends with Snow White, the leading attraction of a cabaret near the station. Snow White was about thirty-five, with long flaxen hair and animated blue eyes. She had been there only a week and was already bored. We had a couple of highballs with her, waltzed her around a few times, treated the orchestra to drinks, all of which came to a phenomenally ridiculous sum, and then we invited her to dinner. A good dinner in a good hotel came to something like seven or eight francs apiece. Snow White, being Swiss, was too dumb, or too good-natured, to hold out for money. She had only one thought in mind—to get back to work on time. It was dark when we left the restaurant. We wandered instinctively towards the edge of the town and soon found an embankment, where we tumbled her over and gave her what's what. She took it like a cocktail, begging us to call for her later in the evening; she would dig up a friend whom she thought we would find attractive. We escorted her back to the cabaret, then set out to explore the town more thoroughly.

In a little café, where an old woman sat playing the zither, we ordered some wine. It was a rather melancholy place, and we were soon bored stiff. As we were about to leave, the proprietor came over and handed us his card, saying that he hoped we would call again. While he was talking, Carl handed me the card and gave me a nudge. I read it. It said, in German, "Café-free-of-Jews." Had it read "Café-free-of-limburger," it could not have struck me as more absurd. We laughed in the man's face. Then I asked him, in French, if he understood English. He said yes. Whereupon I said: "Let me tell you this—though I'm not a Jew, I look on you as an idiot. Haven't you anything better to think of? You're sound asleep . . . You're wallowing in your own shit. *Do you understand that?*" He looked at us bewilderedly. Then Carl began, in a French that would have done credit to an Apache. "Listen, you fucked-out piece of cheese," he began. The man started to raise his voice. "Pipe down," said Carl threateningly, and he made a move as if to throttle the old fool. "I'll say just two words to you: *you're an old cunt. You stink!*" With that he was seized with one of his apoplectic fits of laughter. I think the man had the impression that we were mad. We backed out slowly, laughing hysterically and making grimaces at him. The idiot was so slow-witted, so perplexed, that all he could do was collapse on a chair and mop his brow.

Up the street a little distance we ran across a sleepy-looking policeman. Carl went up to him respectfully, doffed his hat, and, in an impeccable German told him that we had just left the Judenfreies Café where a brawl had started. He urged him to hurry because—here he lowered his voice—the proprietor had taken a fit, he was apt to kill someone. The officer thanked him in his officious, sluggish way and trundled off in the direction of the café. At the corner we found a cab; we

76

asked to be driven to a big hotel which we had spotted earlier in the evening.

We remained in Luxembourg three days, eating and drinking to our heart's content, listening to the excellent orchestras from Germany, observing the quiet, dull life of a people which has no reason to exist, and which in fact does not exist, except as cows or sheep exist. Snow White had introduced us to her friend, who was from Luxembourg and a cretin to the backbone. We talked about making cheese, needlework, country dances, coal mining, exporting and importing, about the royal family and the little ailments which seized them now and then, and so forth. One day we spent entirely in the Valley of the Monks, the Pfaffenthal. A thousand years' peace seemed to reign over this somnolent vale. It was like a corridor which God had traced with his little finger, a reminder to men that when their insatiable thirst for blood had been appeased, when they had become weary of strife, here they would find peace and rest.

To be truthful, it was a beautiful, orderly, prosperous, easy-going sort of world, everyone full of good humor, charitable, kindly, tolerant. Yet, for some reason, there was a rotten odor about the place. The odor of stagnation. The goodness of the inhabitants, which was negative, had deteriorated their moral fiber.

All they were concerned about was to know on which side their bread was buttered. They couldn't make bread, but they could butter it.

I felt thoroughly disgusted. Better to die like a louse in Paris than live here on the fat of the land, thought I to myself.

"Let's go back and get a good dose of clap," I said, rousing Carl from a state of near torpor.

"*What?* What are you talking about?" he mumbled thickly.

"Yes," I said, "let's get out of here, it stinks. Luxembourg is like Brooklyn, only more charming and more poisonous. Let's go back to Clichy and go on a spree. I want to wipe the taste of this out of my mouth."

It was about midnight when we arrived in Paris. We hurried to the newspaper office, where our good friend, King, ran the racing column. We borrowed more francs of him and rushed off.

I was in a mood to take the first whore that came along. "I'll take her, clap and all," thought I. "Shit, a dose of clap is something, after all. Those Luxembourg cunts are full of buttermilk."

Carl wasn't quite so keen about contracting another dose of clap. His cock already felt itchy, he confided. He was trying to think who could have given it to him, if it was the clap, as he suspected.

"If you've got it, there's no great harm in getting it again," I remarked cheerily. "Get a double dose and spread it abroad. Infect the whole continent! Better a good venereal disease than a moribund peace and quiet. Now I know what makes the world civilized: it's vice, disease, thievery, mendacity, lechery. Shit, the French are a great people, even if they're syphilitic. Don't ever ask me to go to a neutral country again. Don't let me look at any more cows, human or otherwise."

I was that peppery I could have raped a nun.

It was in this mood that we entered the little dance hall where our friend, the hat check girl, hung out. It was only a little after midnight, and we had plenty for a little fling. There were three or four whores at the bar and one or two drunks, English, of course. Pansies, most likely. We had a few dances and then the whores began to pester us.

It's amazing what one can do publicly in a French bar. To a *putain* anyone who speaks English, male or female, is a degenerate. A French girl doesn't degrade herself in putting on a show for the foreigner, any more than a sea-lion becomes civilized by being trained to do tricks.

Adrienne, the hat check girl, had come to the bar for a drink. She sat on a high stool with her legs spread apart. I stood beside her with an arm around one of her little friends. Presently I had my hand up her dress. I played with her a little while and then she slid down off her perch and, putting her arms around my neck, stealthily opened my fly and closed her hand over my balls. The musicians were playing a slow waltz, the lights dimmed. Adrienne

80

led me to the floor, my fly wide open, and, holding me tight, she shifted me to the middle of the floor where we were soon packed like sardines. We could hardly move from the spot, the jam was so thick. Again she reached into my fly, took my pecker out, and placed it against her cunt. It was excruciating. To make it more excruciating, one of her little friends who was wedged next to us, brazenly caught hold of my prick. At this point I could hold back no longer—I squirted it into her hand.

When we drifted back to the bar, Carl was standing in a corner, crouched over a girl who seemed to be sagging to the ground. The barman looked annoyed. "This is a drinking place, not a boudoir," he said. Carl looked up in a daze, his face covered with lip rouge, his tie askew, his vest unbuttoned, his hair down over his eyes. "These aren't whores," he muttered, "they're nymphomaniacs."

He sat down on the stool with his shirt tail sticking out of his fly. The girl began buttoning his fly for him. Suddenly she changed her mind, ripped it open again and, pulling his pecker out, bent over and kissed it. This was going a little too far, apparently. The manager now sidled up to inform us that we would have to behave differently or beat it. He didn't appear to be angry with the girls; he simply scolded them, as if they were naughty children.

We were for leaving then and there, but Adrienne insisted that we wait until closing time. She said she wanted to go home with us.

When we finally called a cab and piled in, we discovered that there were five of us. Carl was for shoving one of the girls out, but couldn't make up his mind which one. On the way we stopped to buy some sandwiches, some cheese and olives, and a few bottles of wine.

"They're going to be disappointed when they see how much money we have left," said Carl.

"Good," said I, "maybe they'll all desert us then. I'm tired. I'd like to take a bath and tumble into bed."

As soon as we arrived I undressed and turned on the bath water. The girls were in the kitchen spreading the table. I had just gotten into the tub, and begun soaping myself, when Adrienne and one of the other girls walked into the bathroom. They had decided that they would take a bath too. Adrienne quickly slipped out of her things and slid into the tub with me. The other girl also undressed, then came and stood beside the tub. Adrienne and I were facing each other, our legs entwined. The other girl leaned over the tub and started playing with me. I lay back in the luxuriously hot water and allowed her to twirl her soapy fingers around my cock. Adrienne was playing with her cunt, as if to say—"All right, let her play with that thing a little while, but when the time comes I'll snatch it out of her hand."

Presently the three of us were in the tub, a sandwich in one hand and a glass of wine in the other. Carl had decided to shave. His girl sat on the edge of the *bidet*, chatting and munching her sandwich. She disappeared for a moment to return with a full bottle of red wine which she poured down our necks. The soapy water quickly took on the hue of permanganate.

By this time I was in a mood for anything. Feeling a desire to urinate, I calmly proceeded to pee. The girls were horrified. Apparently I had done something unethical. Suddenly they became suspicious of us. Were we going to pay them? If so, how much? When Carl blithely informed them that he had about nine francs to distribute, there was an uproar. Then they decided that we were only joking—another bad little joke, like peeing in the bathtub. But no, we insisted that we were in earnest. They swore they had never heard the likes of it; it was simply incredible, monstrous, inhuman.

"They're a couple of dirty Huns," said one of the girls.

"No, *English*. Degenerate English," said the other.

Adrienne tried to mollify them. She said she had known us for a long time and that we had always acted like gentlemen with her, an announcement which sounded rather strange to my ears considering the nature of our relations with her. However, the word gentlemen connoted nothing more than that we had always paid cash for her little services.

She was trying desperately to retrieve

the situation. I could almost hear her think.

"Couldn't you give them a check?" she begged.

At this Carl burst out laughing. He was about to say we had no check book when I interrupted him, saying: "Sure, that's an idea . . . we'll give each of you a check, how's that?" I went into Carl's room without another word and got out an old check book of his. I brought him his beautiful Parker pen and handed it to him.

At this point Carl displayed his astuteness. Pretending to be angry with me for having uncovered his check book and for meddling in his affairs, he said:

"It's always like this." (In French, of course, for their benefit.) "I'm the one who always pays for these follies. Why don't you hand out your own checks?"

To this I replied as shamefacedly as I could that my account was dry. Still he demurred, or pretended to.

"Why can't they wait until tomorrow?" he asked, turning to Adrienne. "Won't they trust us?"

"Why should we trust you?" said one of the girls. "A moment ago you pretended you had nothing. Now you want us to wait until tomorrow. Ah, no, that doesn't go with us."

"Well, then, you can all clear out," said Carl, throwing the check book on the floor.

"Don't be so mean," cried Adrienne. "Give us each a hundred francs and we won't speak about it any more. *Please!*"

"A hundred francs *each?*"

"Of course," she said. "That's not very much."

"Go ahead," I said, "don't be such a piker. Besides, I'll pay you back my half in a day or two."

"That's what you always say," Carl replied.

"Cut the comedy," I said, in English. "Write out the checks and let's get rid of them."

"Get rid of them? What, after giving them checks you want me to throw them out? No sir, I'm going to get full value for my money, even if the checks are no good. *They* don't know that. If we let them off too easy they'll smell a rat.

"Hey, *you!*" he shouted, waving a check at one of the girls. "What do I get for this?

I want something unique, not just a lay."

He proceeded to distribute the checks. It looked comical, handing checks around in the raw. Even had they been good, the checks, they looked phony. Possibly because we were all naked. The girls seemed to feel the same way, that it was a phony transaction. Except for Adrienne, who believed in us.

I was praying they'd put on an act rather than force us to go through with the "fucking" routine. I was all in. Dog tired. It would have to be a tall performance, on their part, to make me work up even the semblance of a hard-on. Carl, on the other hand, was behaving like a man who had genuinely doled out three hundred francs. He wanted something for his money, and he wanted something exotic.

While they were talking it over among themselves I climbed into bed. I was so far removed, mentally, from the situation, that I fell into a reverie about the story I had begun days ago and which I intended to resume writing on waking. It was about an axe murder. I wondered if I should attempt to compress the narrative and concentrate on the drunken murderer whom I had left sitting beside the headless body of the wife he had never loved. Perhaps I would take the newspaper account of the crime, telescope it, and begin my own rendition of the murder at the point, or moment, when the head rolled off the table. That would fit in nicely, I thought, with the bit about the armless, legless man who wheeled himself through the streets at night on a little platform, his head on a level with the knees of the passers-by. I wanted a bit of horror because I had a wonderful burlesque up my sleeve which I intended to use as a wind up.

In the brief interval of reverie allotted me I had regained the mood which had been broken days ago by the advent of our somnambulistic Pocahontas.

A nudge from Adrienne, who had made a place for herself beside me, roused me. She was whispering something in my ear. Something about money again. I asked her to repeat it, and, in order not to lose the thought which had just come to me, I kept repeating to myself—"Head rolls off table —head rolls off . . . little man on wheels

. . . wheels . . . legs . . . millions of legs . . ."

"They would like to know if you wouldn't please try to dig up some change for a taxi. They live far away."

"Far away?" I repeated, looking at her vacantly. "How far away?" (*Remember*—wheels, legs, head rolls off . . . begin in the middle of a sentence.)

"Ménilmontant," said Adrienne.

"Get me a pencil and paper—there, on the desk," I begged.

"Ménilmontant . . . Ménilmontant . . ." I repeated hypnotically, scrawling a few key words, such as rubber wheels, wooden heads, corkscrew legs, and so on.

"What are you doing?" hissed Adrienne, tugging at me violently. "What's the matter with you?

"*Il est fou,*" she exclaimed, rising from the bed and throwing up her hands in despair.

"*Où est l'autre?*" she demanded, looking for Carl.

"*Mon Dieu!*" I heard her say, as though from afar, "*il dort.*" Then, after a heavy pause: "Well, that beats everything. Come, let's get out of here! One is drunk and the other is inspired. We're wasting time. That's how foreigners are—always thinking of other things. They don't want to make love, they want to be titillated . . ."

Titillated. I wrote that down, too. I don't remember what she had said in French, but whatever it was, it had resuscitated a forgotten friend. *Titillated.* It was a word I hadn't used for ages. Immediately I thought of another word I only rarely used: *misling.* I was no longer sure what it meant. What matter? I'd drag it in anyway. There were lots of words which had fallen out of my vocabulary, living abroad so long.

I lay back and observed them making ready to leave. It was like watching a stage performance from a box seat. Being a paralytic, I was enjoying the spectacle from my wheelchair. If one of them should take it into her head to throw a pitcher of water over me, I wouldn't stir from the spot. I'd merely shake myself and smile— the way one smiles at frolicsome angels. (Were there such?) All I wanted was for them to go and leave me to my reverie.

Had I had any coins on me I would have flung them at them.

After an aeon or so they made for the door. Adrienne was wafting a long distance kiss, a gesture so unreal that I became fascinated by the poise of her arm; I saw it receding down a long corridor where it was finally sucked through the narrow mouth of a funnel, the arm still bent at the wrist, but so diminished, so attenuated, that it finally resembled a wisp of straw.

"*Salaud!*" shouted one of the girls, and as the door banged shut I caught myself answering: "*Oui, c'est juste. Un salaud. Et vous, des salopes. Il n'y a que ça. N'y a que ça. Salaud, salope. La saloperie, quoi. C'est assoupissant.*"

I snapped out of it with a "Shit, what the hell am I talking about?"

Wheels, legs, head rolling off . . . Fine. Tomorrow will be like any other day, only better, juicier, rosier. The man on the platform will roll himself off the end of a pier. At Canarsie. He will come up with a herring in his mouth. A Maatjes herring, no less.

Hungry again. I got up and looked for the remnants of a sandwich. There wasn't a crumb on the table. I went to the bathroom absent-mindedly, thinking to take a leak. There were a couple of slices of bread, a few pieces of cheese, and some bruised olives scattered about. Thrown away in disgust, evidently.

I picked up a piece of bread to see if it were eatable. Someone had stamped on it with an angry foot. There was a little mustard on it. Or was it mustard? Better try another piece. I salvaged a fairly clean piece, a trifle soggy from lying on the wet floor, and slapped a piece of cheese on it. In a glass beside the *bidet* I found a drop of wine. I downed it, then gingerly bit into the bread. Not bad at all. On the contrary, it tasted good. Germs don't molest hungry people, or inspired people. All rot, this worrying about cellophane and whose hand touched it last. To prove it, I wiped my ass with it. Swiftly, to be sure. Then I gulped it down. *There!* What's to be sorry about? I looked for a cigarette. There were only butts left. I selected the longest one and lit it. Delicious aroma. Not that toasted sawdust from America! Real tobacco. One of Carl's *Gauloises Bleues,* no doubt.

Now what was it I was thinking about?

I sat down at the kitchen table and swung my feet up. Let's see now . . . What was it again?

I couldn't see or think a thing. I felt too absolutely wonderful.

Why think anyway?

Yes, a big day. *Several,* indeed. Yes, it was only a few days ago that we were sitting here, wondering where to go. Might have been yesterday. Or a year ago. What difference? One gets stretched and then one collapses. Time collapses too. Whores collapse. Everything collapses. Collapses into a clap.

On the window-sill an early bird was tweeting. Pleasantly, drowsily, I remembered sitting thus on Brooklyn Heights years ago. In some other life. Would probably never see Brooklyn again. Nor Canarsie, nor Shelter Island, nor Montauk Point, nor Secaucus, nor Lake Pocotopaug, nor the Neversink River, nor scallops and bacon, nor finnan haddie, nor mountain oysters. Strange, how one can stew in the dregs and think it's home. Until someone says Minnehaha—or Walla Walla. *Home.* Home is if home lasts. Where you hang your hat, in other words. Far away, she said, meaning Ménilmontant. That's not far. China now, that's really far. Or Mozambique. Ducky, to drift everlastingly. It's unhealthy, Paris. Maybe she had something there. Try Luxembourg, little one. What the hell, there are thousands of places, Bali, for instance. Or the Carolines. Crazy, this asking for money all the time. Money, money. No money. Lots of money. Yeah, somewhere far, far away. And no books, no typewriter, no nothing. Say nothing, do nothing. Float with the tide. That bitch, Nys. Nothing but a cunt. *What a life!* Don't forget—*titillated!*

I got off my ass, yawned, stretched, staggered to the bed.

Off like a streak. Down, down, to the cosmocentric cesspool. Leviathans swimming around in strangely sunlit depths. Life going on as usual everywhere. Breakfast at ten sharp. An armless, legless man tending bar with his teeth. Dynamite falling through from the stratosphere. Garters descending in long graceful spirals. A woman with a gashed torso struggling desperately to screw her severed head on. Wants money for it. For what? She doesn't know *for what*. Just money. Atop an umbrella fern lies a fresh corpse full of bullet holes. An iron cross is suspended from its neck. Somebody's asking for a sandwich. The water is too agitated for sandwiches. Look under S in the dictionary!

A rich, fecundating dream, shot through with a mystic blue light. I had sunk to that dangerous level where, out of sheer bliss and wonder, one lapses back to the button mold. In some vague dreamy way I was aware that I must make a herculean effort. The struggle to reach the surface was agonizing, exquisitely agonizing. Now and then I succeeded in opening my eyes: I saw the room, as through a mist, but my body was down below in the shimmering marine depths. To swoon back was voluptuous. I fell clear through to the bottomless bottom, where I waited like a shark. Then slowly, very slowly, I rose. It was tantalizing. All cork and no fins. Nearing the surface I was sucked under again, pulled down, down, in delicious helplessness, sucked into the empty vortex, there to wait through endless passages of time for the will to gather and raise me like a sunken buoy.

I awoke with the sound of birds chirping in my ear. The room was no longer veiled in a watery mist but clear and recognizable. On my desk were two sparrows fighting over a crumb. I rested on an elbow and watched them flutter to the window, which was closed. Into the hallway they flew, then back again, frantically seeking an exit.

I got up and opened the window. They continued to fly about the room, as if stunned. I made myself very still. Suddenly they darted through the open window. *"Bonjour, Madame Oursel,"* they cheeped.

It was high noon, about the third or fourth day of spring . . .

—Henry Miller
New York City,
June, 1940.
Rewritten in Big Sur, May, 1956.

MARA-MARIGNAN

It was near the Café Marignan on the Champs-Elysées that I ran into her.

I had only recently recovered from a painful separation from Mara-St. Louis. That was not her name, but let us call her that for the moment, because it was on the Ile St. Louis that she was born, and it was there I often walked about at night, letting the rust eat into me.

It is because I heard from her just the other day, after giving her up for lost, that I am able to recount what follows. Only now, because of certain things which have become clear to me for the first time, the story has grown more complicated.

I might say, in passing, that my life seems to have been one long search for *the* Mara who would devour all the others and give them significant reality.

The Mara who precipitated events was neither the Mara of the Champs-Elysées nor the Mara of the Ile St. Louis. The Mara I speak of was called Eliane. She was married to a man who had been jailed for passing counterfeit money. She was also the mistress of my friend Carl, who had at first been passionately in love with her and who was now, on this afternoon I speak of, so bored with her that he couldn't tolerate the thought of going to see her alone.

Eliane was young, slim, attractive, except that she was liberally peppered with moles and had a coat of down on her upper lip. In the eyes of my friend these blemishes at first only enhanced her beauty, but as he grew tired of her their presence irritated him and sometimes caused him to make caustic jokes which made her wince. When she wept she became, strangely enough, more beautiful than ever. With her face wreathed in tears she looked the mature woman, not the slender androgynous creature with whom Carl had fallen in love.

Eliane's husband and Carl were old friends. They had met in Budapest, where the former had rescued Carl from starvation and later had given him the money to go to Paris. The gratitude which Carl first entertained for the man soon changed to contempt and ridicule when he discovered how stupid and insensitive the fellow was. Ten years later they met by chance on the street in Paris. The invitation to dinner, which followed, Carl would never have accepted had the husband not flaunted a photograph of his young wife. Carl was immediately infatuated. She reminded him, he informed me, of a girl named Marcienne, about whom he was writing at the time.

I remember well how the story of Marcienne blossomed as his clandestine meeting with Eliane became more and more frequent. He had seen Marcienne only three or four times after their meeting in the forest of Marly where he had stumbled upon her in the company of a beautiful greyhound. I mention the dog because, when he was first struggling with the story, the dog had more reality (for me) than the woman with whom he was supposed to be in love. With Eliane's entrance into his life the figure of Marcienne began to take on form and substance; he even endowed Marcienne with one of Eliane's superfluous moles, the one at the nape of her neck, which he said made him particularly passionate every time he kissed it.

For some months now he had the pleasure of kissing all Eliane's beautiful moles, including the one on the left leg, up near the crotch. They no longer made him inflammatory. He had finished the story of Marcienne and, in doing so, his passion for Eliane had evaporated.

The finishing stroke was the husband's arrest and conviction. While the husband was at large there had been at least the excitement of danger; now that he was safely behind the bars, Carl was faced with a mistress who had two children to support and who very naturally looked to him as a protector and provider. Carl was not ungenerous but he certainly was not a provider. He was rather fond of children, too, I must say, but he didn't like to play the father to the children of a man whom he despised. Under the circumstances the best thing he could think of was to find Eliane a job, which he proceeded to do. When he was broke he ate with her. Now and then he complained that she worked too hard, that she was ruining her beauty; secretly, of course, he was pleased, because an Eliane worn with fatigue made less demands on his time.

The day he persuaded me to accompany him he was in a bad mood. He had received a telegram from her that morning, saying that she was free for the day and that he should come as early as possible. He decided to go about four in the afternoon and leave with me shortly after dinner. I was to think up some excuse which would enable him to withdraw without creating a scene.

When we arrived I found that there were three children instead of two—he had forgotten to tell me that there was a baby too. A pure oversight, he remarked. I must say the atmosphere wasn't precisely that

of a love nest. The baby carriage was
standing at the foot of the steps in the
dingy courtyard, and the brat was scream-
ing at the top of its lungs. Inside, the
children's clothes were hanging up to dry.
The windows were wide open and there
were flies everywhere. The oldest child was
calling him daddy, which annoyed him beyond measure. In a surly voice he told
Eliane to pack the kids off. This almost
provoked a burst of tears. He threw me
one of those helpless looks which said:
"It's begun already . . . how am I ever
going to survive the ordeal?" And then, in
desperation, he began to pretend that he
was quite merry, calling for drinks, bounc-
ing the kids on his knee, reciting poetry to
them, patting Eliane on the rump, briskly
and disinterestedly, as though it were a
private ham which he had ordered for the
occasion. He even went a little further, in
his simulated gayety; with glass in hand he
beckoned Eliane to approach, first giving
her a kiss on his favorite mole, and then,
urging me to draw closer, he put his free
hand in her blouse and fished up one of

her teats, which he coolly asked me to appraise.

I had witnessed these performances before—with other women whom he had been in love with. His emotions usually went through the same cycle: passion, coolness, indifference, boredom, mockery, contempt, disgust. I felt sorry for Eliane. The presence of the children, the poverty, the drudgery, the humiliation, rendered the situation far from funny. Seeing that the jest had missed fire, Carl suddenly felt ashamed of himself. He put his glass down and, with the look of a beaten dog, he put his arms around her and kissed her on the forehead. That was to indicate that she was still an angel, even if her rump were appetizing and the left breast exceedingly tempting. Then a silly grin spread over his face and he sat himself down on the divan, muttering Yah, Yah, as though to say— "That's how things are, it's sad, but what can you do?"

To relieve the tension, I volunteered to take the children out for a walk, the one in the carriage included. At once Carl became alarmed. He didn't want me to go for a walk. From the gestures and grimaces he was making behind Eliane's back, I gathered that he didn't relish the idea of performing his amorous duties just yet. Aloud he was saying that *he* would take the kids for an airing; behind her back he was making me to understand, by deaf and dumb gestures, that he wanted *me* to take a crack at her, Eliane. Even had I wanted to, I couldn't. I didn't have the heart for it. Besides, I felt more inclined to torture him because of the callous way in which he was treating her. Meanwhile the children, having caught the drift of the conversation, and having witnessed the deaf and dumb show behind their mother's back, began to act as if the very devil had taken possession of them. They pleaded and begged, then bellowed and stamped their feet in uncontrollable rage. The infant in the carriage began to squawk again, the parrot set up a racket, the dog started yelping. Seeing that they couldn't have their way, the brats began to imitate Carl's antics, which they had studied with amusement and mystification. Their gestures were thoroughly obscene, and poor Eliane was at a loss to know what had come over them.

By this time Carl had grown hysterical. To Eliane's amazement, he suddenly began to repeat his dumb antics openly, this time as though imitating the children. At this point I could no longer control myself. I began to howl with laughter, the children following suit. Then, to silence Eliane's remonstrances, Carl pushed her over on the divan, making the most god-awful grimaces at her while he chattered like a monkey in that Austrian dialect which she loathed. The children piled on top of her, screeching like guinea hens, and making obscene gestures which she was powerless to hinder because Carl had begun to tickle her and bite her neck, her legs, her rump, her breasts. There she was, her skirts up to her neck, wriggling, squealing, laughing as if she would burst, and at the same time furious, almost beside herself. When she at last managed to disengage herself she broke into violent sobs. Carl sat beside her, looking distraught, baffled, and muttering as before—Yah, Yah. I quietly took the youngsters by the hand and led them out into the courtyard, where I amused them as best I could while the two lovers patched things up.

When I returned I found that they had moved into the adjoining room. They were so quiet I thought at first that they had fallen asleep. But suddenly the door opened and Carl stuck his head out, giving me his usual clownish grin, which meant—"All's clear, I gave her the works." Eliane soon appeared, looking flushed and smolderingly content. I lay down on the divan and played with the kids while Carl and Eliane went out to buy food for the evening meal. When they returned they were in high spirits. I suspected that Carl, who beamed at the mere mention of food, must have been carried away by his enthusiasm and promised Eliane things which he had no intention of fulfilling. Eliane was strangely gullible; it was probably the fault of the moles, which were a constant reminder that her beauty was not untarnished. To pretend to love her because of her moles, which was undoubtedly Carl's line of approach, rendered her hopelessly defenseless. Anyway she was becoming more and more radiant. We had another *Amer Picon,* one too many for her, and then, as the twilight slowly faded, we began to sing.

In such moods we always sang German songs. Eliane sang too, though she despised the German tongue. Carl was a different fellow now. No longer panicky. He had probably given her a successful lay, he had had three or four *apéritifs,* he was ravenously hungry. Besides night was coming on, and he would soon be free. In short, the day was progressing satisfactorily in every way.

When Carl became mellow and expansive, he was irresistible. He talked glowingly about the wine he had bought, a very expensive wine which, on such occasions, he always insisted he had bought expressly for me. While talking about the wine he began devouring the *hors d'œuvre.* That made him more thirsty. Eliane tried to restrain him, but there was no holding him back now. He fished out one of her teats again, this time without protest on her part, and, after pouring a little wine over it, he nibbled at it greedily—to the children's huge enjoyment. Then, of course, he had to show me the mole on her left leg, up near the crotch. From the way things were going on, I thought they were going back to the bedroom again, but no, suddenly he put her teat back inside her blouse and sat down saying: *"J'ai faim, j'ai faim, chérie."* In tone it was no different than his usual "Fuck me, dearie, I can't wait another second!"

During the course of the meal, which was excellent, we got on to some strange topics. When eating, especially if he enjoyed the food, Carl always kept up a rambling conversation which permitted him to concentrate on the food and wine. In order to avoid the dangers of a serious discussion, one which would interfere with his digestive processes, he would throw out random remarks of a nature he thought suitable and appropriate for the morsel of food, or the glass of wine, he was about to gulp down. In this off-hand way he blurted out that he had just recently met a girl—he wasn't sure if she were a whore or not, what matter?—whom he was thinking of introducing me to. Before I could ask why, he added—"She's just your type.

"I know your type," he rattled on, making a quick allusion to Mara of the Ile St. Louis. "This one is much better," he added. "I'm going to fix it for you . . ."

Often, when he said a thing like this, he had nobody in mind. He would say it because the idea of presenting me to some mythical beauty had just popped into his head. There was this about it also, that he had never liked what he called "my type." When he wanted to sting me he would insinuate that there were thousands of such types floating about in Central Europe, and that only an American would find such a woman attractive. If he wanted to be downright nasty he would inject a little sarcasm of this sort: "This one isn't under thirty-five, I can promise you that." Sometimes, as on the present occasion, I would pretend to believe his story and ply him with questions, which he would answer flippantly and vaguely. Now and then, however, especially if I taunted him, he would embellish the story with such convincing details that in the end he seemed to believe his own lie. At such moments he would assume a truly demonic expression, inventing with a rapidity that was like wild-fire the most extraordinary conversations and happenings. In order not to lose the reins he would make frequent attacks on the bottle, tossing a tall drink off as if it were so much froth, but with each toss of the head growing more and more purple, the veins standing out on his forehead in knots, his voice becoming more frantic, his gestures more uncontrolled, and his eyes piercing, as if he were hallucinated. Coming to an abrupt halt, he would look about with a wild eye, make a dramatic gesture of pulling out his watch, and then in a calm, matter of fact voice, say: "In ten minutes she'll be standing at the corner of such and such a street; she's wearing a dotted Swiss dress and has a porcupine handbag under her arm. If you want to meet her, go and see for yourself." And with that he'd nonchalantly switch the conversation to a remote subject—*since he had offered us proof of the truth of his words*. Usually of course nobody budged to verify these astounding statements. "You're afraid to," he would say. "You know that she'll be standing there . . ." And with this he would add another striking detail, quite casually, always in a matter of fact voice, as though he were transmitting a message from the other world.

In predictions which were more immediately verifiable, which didn't involve breaking up a good meal, or an evening's entertainment, he was so often correct that, when these performances got under way, his auditors usually felt something like a cold chill running down their spines. What began as something clownish and flippant often turned into something horrible and uncanny. If the new moon were out, and these attacks of his often coincided with certain lunar phases, as I had occasions to observe, the evening would become shudderingly grotesque. To catch a glimpse of the moon unexpectedly would completely unnerve him. "There it is!" he would shriek—exactly as if he had seen a ghost. "It's bad, it's bad," he would mumble over and over, rubbing his hands frantically, then pace up and down the room with head lowered, his mouth half open, his tongue protruding like a piece of red flannel.

Fortunately, on this occasion there was no moon, or if there were, its maddening gleams had not yet penetrated the court-yard of Eliane's little home. His exaltation had no worse effect upon him than to launch him into a long story about Eliane's foolish husband. It was a ridiculous story, quite true, as I found out later. About a pair of dachshunds which the husband had looked upon with a covetous eye. He had seen them running about loose, the owner nowhere in sight, and, not content with palming off counterfeit bills successfully, he had decided to steal the dogs and de-mand a ransom for their recovery. When he answered the door bell one morning, and found a French detective waiting for him, he was dumfounded. He had just been feeding the dogs their breakfast. In fact he had become so attached to the dogs that he had forgotten all about the reward which he was hoping to capture. He thought it a cruel stroke of fate to be arrested for being kind to animals . . . The affair reminded Carl of other incidents which he had witnessed when living with the man in Budapest. They were silly, ridiculous incidents which could occur only in the life of a half-wit, as Carl dubbed him.

By the time the meal was over Carl felt so good that he decided to have a little snooze. When I saw that he had fallen sound asleep I paid my respects to Eliane and bolted. I had no particular desire to go anywhere; I strolled over to the Etoile, which was only a few blocks away, and then instinctively headed down the Champs-Elysees in the direction of the Tuileries, thinking to stop somewhere along the line and have a black coffee. I felt mellow, expansive and at peace with the world. The glitter and frou-frou of the Champs-Elysées contrasted strangely with the atmosphere of the courtyard, where the baby carriage was still parked. I was not only well fed, well oiled, but well shod and well groomed, for a change. I remember having paid to have my shoes shined earlier in the day.

Strolling along the broad boulevard, I suddenly recalled my first visit to the

Champs-Elysées, some five or six years pre-
vious. I had been to the cinema and, feeling
rather good, I had struck out for the
Champs-Elysées to have a quiet drink before turning in. At a little bar on one of
the side streets I had had several drinks all
by myself. While drinking I had taken to
thinking of an old friend of mine in Brooklyn, and how wonderful it would be if he
were with me. I carried on quite a conversation with him, in my mind; in fact, I
was still talking to him as I swung into the
Champs-Elysées. Somewhat cockeyed, and
extremely exalted, I was bewildered when I
saw all the trees. I looked about in puzzled
fashion, then made a bee-line for the café
lights. As I neared the Marignan an attrac-
tive-looking whore, brisk, voluble, dom-
ineering, grabbed my arm and started to
accompany me. I knew only about ten
words of French then and, what with the
dazzling lights, the profusion of trees, the
spring fragrance and the warm glow inside
me, I was completely helpless. I knew I
was in for it. I knew I was going to be
trimmed. Lamely I tried to call a halt, tried
to come to some understanding with her. I

remember that we were standing directly in front of the *terrasse* of the Marignan, which was alive and swarming with people. I remember that she got between me and the crowd and, keeping up a patter which was altogether beyond me, unbuttoned my overcoat and made a grab for it. All this while making the most suggestive grimaces with her lips. Any feeble resistance I had intended to offer broke down at once. In a few minutes we were in a hotel room and before I could say Gallagher, she was sucking me off in expert fashion, having stripped me first of everything but the loose change in my coat pocket.

I was thinking of this incident and of the ludicrous trips to the American Hospital in Neuilly some few days later (to cure an imaginary case of syphilis), when suddenly I noticed a girl in front of me turning round to catch my eye. She stood there waiting for me to approach, as though absolutely certain that I would take her by the arm and continue strolling down the avenue. Which is exactly what I did. I don't think I even paused as I caught up with her. It seemed the most natural thing in the world to say, in answer to the usual "Hello, where are you strolling?"— "Why nowhere, let's sit down somewhere and have a drink."

My readiness, my nonchalance, my insouciance, coupled with the fact that I was well groomed, well shod, could well have given her the impression that I was an American millionaire. As we approached the glittering lights of the café, I noticed that it was the Marignan. Though there was no longer any need for shade, the parasols were standing open above the tables. The girl was rather lightly clad and wore about her neck the typical badge of the whore. Hers was a rather frowsy piece of fur, rather worn and moth-eaten, it seemed to me. I paid little attention to anything except her eyes, which were hazel and extremely beautiful. They reminded me of someone, someone I had once been in love with. Who it was I couldn't recall at the moment.

For some reason Mara, as she called herself, was dying to talk English. It was an English which she had picked up in Costa Rica, where she had run a night

club, so she said. It was the first time, in all
the years I had been in Paris, that a whore
had expressed a desire to talk English. She
was doing so apparently because it reminded her of the good times she had had
in Costa Rica, where she had been something better than a whore. And then there
was another reason—Mr. Winchell. Mr.
Winchell was a charming, generous American, *a gentleman,* she said, whom she had
run across in Paris after returning from
Costa Rica penniless and heart-broken.
Mr. Winchell belonged to some athletic
club in New York and, even though he had
his wife in tow, he had treated her swell.
In fact, gentleman that he was, Mr. Winchell had introduced Mara to his wife, and
together the three of them had gone to
Deauville on a lark. So she said. There may
have been some truth in it, because there
are fellows like Winchell floating about,
and now and then, in their enthusiasm,
they pick up a whore and treat her like a
lady. And sometimes the little whore can
really be a lady. But as Mara was saying,
this man Winchell was a prince—and his
wife wasn't a bad sort, either. Naturally,

when Mr. Winchell proposed sleeping three abed, the wife got sore. But Mara didn't blame her for that. *"Elle avait raison,"* she said.

However, Mr. Winchell was gone now, and the check he had left Mara on leaving for America had long ago been eaten up. It had gone fast because, as things turned out, no sooner had Mr. Winchell disappeared than Ramon turned up. Ramon had been in Madrid, trying to get a cabaret started, but then the revolution had broken out and Ramon had to flee, and of course when he arrived in Paris he was dead broke. Ramon was also a good guy, according to Mara. She trusted him absolutely. But now he was gone too. She didn't know quite where he had disappeared to. She was certain, however, that he would send for her one day. She was dead sure of it, though she hadn't had word from him for over a year now.

All this while the coffee was being served. In that strange English which because of her low, hoarse voice, her pathetic earnestness, her obvious effort to please me (perhaps I was another Mr. Winchell?),

118

moved me strongly. There was a pause, a rather long pause, during which I suddenly thought of Carl's words at dinner. She was indeed "my type" and, though he hadn't made any such prophecy this time, she was precisely the sort of creature whom he might have described for me on the impulse of the moment while dramatically pulling out his watch and saying—"in ten minutes she will be on the corner of such and such a street."

"What are you doing here in Paris?" she asked in an effort to get on more familiar ground. And then, as I started to answer, she interrupted me to inquire if I were hungry. I told her I had just had a marvelous meal. I suggested that we have a liqueur and another coffee. Suddenly I noticed that she was looking at me intently, almost uncomfortably so. I had the impression that she was thinking of Mr. Winchell again, perhaps comparing me with him or identifying me with him, perhaps thanking God for having sent her another American *gentleman* and not a hard-headed Frenchman. It seemed unfair to let her mind travel on in this vein, if that were really her train of thought. So, as gently as possible, I let her know that I was by no means a millionaire.

At this point she suddenly leaned over and confessed to me that she was hungry, very hungry. I was astounded. It was long past dinner hour and besides, stupid though it be, I had simply never thought of a Champs-Elysées whore suffering from hunger. I also felt somewhat ashamed of myself for being so thoughtless as not to inquire if she had eaten. "Why not go inside?" I suggested, taking it for granted that she would be delighted to eat at the Marignan. Most women if hungry, particularly if *very* hungry, would have accepted the suggestion at once. But this one shook her head. She wouldn't think of eating at the Marignan—it was too expensive. I told her to forget what I had said a moment ago, about not being a millionaire and all that, but she remained adamant. She preferred to seek out some ordinary little restaurant, she didn't care where—there were plenty of them nearby, she said. I pointed out that it was past closing time for most restaurants, but she insisted that we look nevertheless. And then, as if she had forgotten all about her hunger, she drew closer, squeezed my hand warmly, and began telling me what a swell guy she thought I was. With this she began all over again the story of her life in Costa Rica and other places in the Caribbean, places I couldn't imagine a girl like her living in. Finally it boiled down to this, that she wasn't cut out to be a whore and never would be. If I could believe her, she was utterly sick of it.

"You're the first man in a long time," she went on, "who's treated me like a human being. I want you to know that it's a privilege just to sit and talk with you." At this point she had a twinge of hunger and, shivering a bit, she tried to wrap the crazy, skinny fur tighter about her neck. Her arms were covered with goose pimples and there was something incongruous about her smile, something too brave and nonchalant about it. I didn't wish to detain her a moment longer than necessary, but despite my readiness to go she continued to talk—a compulsive, hysterical flow of speech which, though it had nothing to do with hunger, made me think of the food she needed and which I feared she might pass up after all.

"The man who gets me gets pure gold," I suddenly heard her exclaim, and then her hands were lying on the table, palms up. She begged me to study them.

"That is what life can do to you!" she murmured.

"But you're beautiful," I said, warmly and sincerely. "I don't care about your hands."

She insisted that she wasn't beautiful, adding, "But I *was* once. Now I'm tired, worn out. I want to get away from all this. *Paris!* It looks beautiful, doesn't it? But it stinks, I tell you. I've always worked for a living . . . Look, look at my hands again! But *here*, here they won't let you work. They want to suck the blood out of you. *Je suis française, moi, mais je n'aime pas mes compatriotes; ils sont durs, méchants, sans pitié pour nous.*"

I stopped her gently to remind her of dinner. Hadn't we better be getting along? She agreed absent-mindedly, still smoldering with resentment towards her callous compatriots. But she did not budge. Instead she scanned the terrace searchingly. I was wondering what had come over her when suddenly she got to her feet and, bending over me solicitously, she asked if I would mind waiting a few minutes. She had a rendezvous, she hurriedly explained, with some old geezer at a café just up the street. She didn't think he would be there anymore, but just the same it was worth investigating. If he were there it would mean a little jack. Her thought was to make it a quick one and rejoin me as soon as possible. I told her not to worry about me. "Take your time and get what you can out of the old buzzard. I have nothing to do," I added. "I'll sit here and wait. You're going to have dinner with me, remember that."

I watched her sail up the avenue and duck into the café. I doubted that she would return. *Rich geezer!* It was more likely her *maquereau* she was running off to mollify. I could see him telling her what a dope she must be to accept a dinner engagement with a fool American. He would buy her a sandwich and a beer, and out she'd go again. If she protested, she'd get a sound slap in the face.

To my surprise she was back in less than ten minutes. She seemed disappointed and not disappointed. "It's rare for a man to keep his word," she said. Excepting Mr. Winchell, of course. Mr. Winchell was different. "He always kept his word," she said. "Until he left for America."

Mr. Winchell's silence genuinely perplexed her. He had promised to write regularly, but it was over three months since he had left and she hadn't had a line from him. She rummaged through her bag to see if she could find his card. Perhaps if I wrote a letter for her, in my English, it would bring a response. The card had been mislaid apparently. She remembered, though, that he lived at some athletic club in New York. His wife lived there too, she said. The *garçon* came and she ordered another black coffee. It was eleven o'clock or more, and I was wondering where at that hour we would find a cozy, inexpensive restaurant such as she had in mind.

I was still thinking of Mr. Winchell, and what a strange athletic club he must be stopping at, when I heard her say as if from far off—"Listen, I don't want you to spend a lot of money on me. I hope you're *not* rich; I don't care about your money. It does me good just to talk to you. You don't know how it feels to be treated like a human being!" And then it broke out again, about Costa Rica and the other places, the men she had given herself to, and how it didn't matter because she had loved them; they would always remember her because when she gave herself to a man she gave herself body and soul. Again she looked at her hands, and then she smiled wanly and wrapped the stringy fur tight about her throat.

No matter how much of it was invention, I knew her feelings were honest and true. Thinking to make the situation a little easier for her I suggested, perhaps too abruptly, that she accept what money I had on me and we'd say good-bye then and there. I was trying to let her know that I didn't want to hang on and make her feel grateful for a little thing like a meal. I insinuated that perhaps she would prefer being alone. Maybe she ought to go off by herself, get drunk, and have a good cry. I blurted it out as delicately and tactfully as I could.

Still she made no effort to go. A struggle was going on inside her. She had forgotten that she was cold and hungry. Undoubtedly she had identified me with other men she had loved, those to whom she had given herself body and soul—and who would always remember her, as she said.

The situation was getting so delicate that I begged her to talk French; I didn't want to hear her mutilate the beautiful, tender things she was spilling out by translating them into a grotesque Costa Rica English.

"I tell you," she blurted out, "had it been any other man but you I would have stopped talking English long ago. It tires me to talk English. But now I don't feel tired at all. I think it is beautiful to talk English to someone who understands you. Sometimes I go with a man and he never talks to me at all. He doesn't want to know *me, Mara*. He doesn't care about anything except my body. What can I give a man like that? Feel me, how hot I am . . . I'm burning up."

126

In the cab, going towards the Avenue Wagram, she seemed to lose her bearings. "Where are you taking me?" she demanded, as if we were already in some unknown and outlandish section of the city. "Why, we're just nearing the Avenue Wagram," I said. "What's the matter with you?" She looked around bewilderedly, as though she had never heard of such a street. Then, seeing the somewhat astonished expression on my face, she drew me close and bit me on the mouth. She bit hard, like an animal. I held her tight and slipped my tongue down her throat. My hand was on her knee; I pulled her dress up and slid my hand over the hot flesh. She started to bite again, first the mouth, then the neck, then the ear. Suddenly she pulled herself out of the embrace, saying—"*Mon Dieu, attendez un peu, attendez, je vous en prie.*"

We had already gone past the place I had in mind to take her. I leaned forward and told the driver to turn back. When we stepped out of the cab she seemed dazed. It was a big café, on the order of the Marignan, and there was an orchestra playing. I had to coax her to go inside.

As soon as she had ordered her food she excused herself and went downstairs to tidy up. When she came back I noticed for the first time how shabby her clothes were. I was sorry that I had forced her to come to such a brilliantly lit place. While waiting for the veal cutlet which she had ordered she got out a long file and began to manicure her nails. The varnish had worn off some of the nails, making her fingers look even uglier than they were. The soup came and she laid the nail file aside temporarily. Her comb she put beside the nail file. I buttered a slice of bread for her and, when I handed it to her, she blushed. She swallowed the soup hastily, then tackled the bread, gobbling down big chunks of it with head down, as if ashamed to be seen eating so ravenously. Suddenly she looked up and, taking my hand impulsively, she said in a low, confiding voice: "Listen, Mara never forgets. The way you talked to me tonight—I'll never forget that. It was better than if you had given me a thousand francs. Look, we haven't spoken about this yet, *but*—if you'd like to go with me . . . I mean . . ."

"Suppose we don't talk about that now," I said. "I don't mean that I don't *want* to go with you. But . . ."

"I understand," she blurted impetuously. "I don't want to spoil your beautiful gesture. I understand what you mean, *but*— anytime you want to see Mara"—and she began to fumble through her bag—"I mean that you don't ever have to *give* me anything. Couldn't you call me up tomorrow? Why not let me take *you* to dinner?"

She was still searching for a piece of paper. I tore off a bit of the paper napkin; she wrote down her name and address in a large scrawling hand with the blunt stump of a pencil. It was a Polish name. The name of the street I didn't recognize. "It's in the St. Paul quarter," she said. "Please don't come to the hotel," she added, "I'm only living there temporarily."

I looked at the name of the street again. I thought I knew the St. Paul quarter well. The more I looked at the name the more I was convinced that there was no such street, not in any part of Paris. However, one can't remember the name of every street. . . .

"So you're Polish, then?"

"No, I'm a Jewess. I was *born* in Poland. Anyway, that's not my real name."

I said nothing more; the subject died as quickly as it had been born.

As the meal progressed I became aware of the attention of a man opposite us. He was an elderly Frenchman who appeared to be engrossed in his paper; every now and then however, I caught his eye as he peered over the edge of the paper to give Mara the once—over. He had a kindly face and seemed rather well-to-do. I sensed that Mara had already sized him up.

I was curious to know what she would do if I slipped away for a few moments. So, after the coffee had been ordered, I excused myself and went downstairs to the *lavabo*. When I returned I could tell by the quiet, easy way she was puffing at her cigarette that things had been arranged. The man was now thoroughly absorbed in his newspaper. There seemed to be a tacit agreement that he would wait until she had done with me.

When the waiter came by I asked what time it was. Almost one, he said. "It's late,

Mara, I must be going," said I. She laid her hand on mine and looked up at me with a knowing smile. "You don't have to play that game with me," she said. "I know why you left the table. Really, you're so kind, I don't know how to thank you. Please don't run away. It isn't necessary, he will wait. I told him to . . . Look, let me walk with you a little way. I want a few more words with you before we part, yes?"

We walked down the street in silence. "You're not angry with me, are you?" she asked, clutching my arm.

"No, Mara, I'm not angry. Of course not."

"Are you in love with someone?" she asked, after a pause.

"Yes, Mara, I am."

She was silent again. We walked on for another block or so in eloquent silence and then, as we came to an unusually dark street, she hugged my arm still tighter and whispered . . . "Come this way." I let her steer me down the dark street. Her voice grew huskier, the words rushing out of her mouth pell-mell. I haven't the slightest recollection now of what she said, nor do

131

I think she herself knew when the flood broke from her lips. She talked wildly, frantically, against a fatality that was overpowering. Whoever she was, she no longer had a name. She was just a woman, bruised, badgered, broken, a creature beating its helpless wings in the dark. She wasn't addressing anyone, least of all *me;* she wasn't talking to herself either, nor to God. She was just a babbling wound that had found a voice, and in the darkness the wound seemed to open up and create a space around itself in which it could bleed without shame or humiliation. All the while she kept clutching my arm, as if to verify my presence; she pressed it with her strong fingers, as if the touch of her fingers would convey the meaning which her words no longer contained.

In the midst of this bleeding babble she suddenly stopped dead. "Put your arms around me," she begged. "Kiss me, kiss me like you did in the cab." We were standing near the doorway of a huge, deserted mansion. I moved her up against the wall and put my arms around her in a mad embrace. I felt her teeth brush against my ear. She had her arms locked around my waist; she pulled me to her with all her strength. Passionately she murmured: "Mara knows how to love. Mara will do anything for you . . . *Embrassez-moi!* . . . *Plus fort, plus fort, chéri* . . ." We stood there in the doorway clutching one another, groaning, mumbling incoherent phrases. Someone was approaching with heavy, ominous steps. We pulled apart and, without a word, I shook hands with her and walked off. After I had gone a few yards, moved by the absolute silence of the street, I turned around. She was standing where I had left her. We remained motionless several minutes, straining to see through the darkness. Then impulsively I walked back to her.

"Look here, Mara," I said, "supposing he's not there?"

"Oh, he'll be there," she answered, in a toneless voice.

"Listen, Mara," I said, "you'd better take this . . . just in case," and I fished out the contents of my pocket and stuffed it in her hand. I turned and walked off rapidly, throwing a gruff "*au revoir*" over my shoulder. That's that, I thought to myself, and hastened my steps a little. The next moment I heard someone running behind me. I turned to find her on top of me, breathless. She threw her arms around me again, mumbling some extravagant words of thanks. Suddenly I felt her body slump. She was trying to slide to her knees. I yanked her up brusquely and, holding her by the waist at arm's length, I said: "Christ Almighty, what's the matter with you—hasn't anybody ever treated you decently?" I said it almost angrily. The next moment I could have bitten my tongue out. She stood there in the dark street with her hands to her face, her head bowed, sobbing to break her heart. She was trembling from head to toe. I wanted to put my arms around her; I wanted to say something that would comfort her, but I couldn't. I was paralyzed. Suddenly, like a frightened horse, I bolted. Faster and faster I walked, her sobs still ringing in my ears. I went on and on, faster, faster, like a crazed antelope, until I came to a blaze of lights.

"She will be at the corner of such and

*such a street in ten minutes; she will be
wearing a red dotted Swiss dress and she
will have a porcupine handbag under her
arm . . ."*

Carl's words kept repeating themselves
in my brain. I looked up, and there was
the moon, not silvery but mercurial. It was
swimming in a sea of frozen fat. Round
and round and round as if it were huge,
terrifying rings of blood. I stood stock still.
I shuddered. And then suddenly, without
warning, like a great gout of blood, a terrifying sob broke loose. I wept like a child.

A few days later I was strolling through
the Jewish quarter. There was no such
street as she had given me in the St. Paul
district, nor anywhere in Paris. I consulted
the telephone book to find that there were
several hotels by the name she had given,
but none of them were anywhere in the
vicinity of St. Paul. I was not surprised,
merely perplexed. To be honest, I had
thought little about her since I had taken
flight down that dark street.

I had told Carl about the affair, of
course. There were two things he said, on

hearing the story, which stuck in my crop.

"I suppose you know whom she reminded you of?"

When I said no, he laughed. "Think it over," he said, "you'll remember."

The other remark was this, which was typical of him: "I knew that you would meet someone. I wasn't asleep when you left; I was only pretending. If I had told you what was going to happen you would have taken another direction, just to prove me wrong."

It was a Saturday afternoon when I went over to the Jewish quarter. I had started out for the Place des Vosges, which I still regard as one of the most beautiful spots in Paris. It being a Saturday, however, the square was filled with children. The Place des Vosges is a spot to go to at night, when you are absolutely tranquil and eager to enjoy solitude. It was never meant to be a playground; it is a place of memories, a silent, healing place, in which to gather one's forces.

As I was going through the archway leading to the Faubourg St. Antoine, Carl's words came back to me. And at the same instant I recalled whom it was Mara resembled. It was Mara-St. Louis, whom I had known as Christine. We had driven here in a carriage one evening before going to the station. She was leaving for Copenhagen and I was never to see her again. It was *her* idea to revisit the Place des Vosges. Knowing that I came here frequently on my lonely nocturnal rambles, she had thought to bequeath me the memory of a last embrace in this beautiful square where she had played as a child. Never before had she mentioned anything about this place in connection with her childhood. We had always talked about the Ile St. Louis; we had often gone to the house where she was born, and had often walked through the narrow isle at night on our way home from a gathering, always stopping for a moment in front of the old house to look up at the window where she had sat as a child.

Since there was a good hour or more to kill before train time, we had dismissed the carriage and sat at the curb near the old archway. An unusual atmosphere of gayety prevailed this particular evening;

people were singing, and children were dancing about the tables, clapping their hands, stumbling over the chairs, falling and picking themselves up good-naturedly. Christine began to sing for me—a little song which she had learned as a child. People recognized the air and joined in. Never did she look more beautiful. It was hard to believe that she would soon be on the train—and out of my life forever. We were so gay on leaving the Place that one would have thought we were going off on a honeymoon . . .

At the Rue des Rosiers, in the Jewish quarter, I stopped at the little shop near the synagogue, where they sell herrings and sour pickles. The fat, rosy-cheeked girl who usually greeted me was not there. It was she who had told me one day, when Christine and I were together, that we should get married quickly or we would regret it.

"She's married already," I had said laughingly.

"But not to *you!*"

"Do you think we would be happy together?"

"You will never be happy unless together. You are meant for one another; you must never leave each other, no matter what happens."

I walked about the neighborhood, thinking of this strange colloquy, and wondering what had become of Christine. Then I thought of Mara sobbing in the dark street, and for a moment I had an uncomfortable, crazy thought—that, perhaps at that very moment when I was tearing myself away from Mara, Christine was also sobbing in her sleep in some dreary hotel room. From time to time rumors had reached me that she was no longer with her husband, that she had taken to wandering from place to place, always on her own. She had never written me a line. For her it was a final separation. "Forever," she had said. Still, as I walked about at night thinking of her, whenever I stopped before the old house on the Ile St. Louis and looked up at the window, it seemed unbelievable that she had relinquished me forever, in mind and heart. We should have taken the fat girl's advice and married, that was the sad truth. If I could only have divined where she was, I would have taken a train and gone to her, immediately. Those sobs in the dark, they rang in my ears. How could I know that she, Christine, was not sobbing too, now, this very moment? *What time was it!* I began to think of strange cities where it was night now, or early morning: lonely, God-forsaken places, where women bereft and abandoned were shedding tears of woe. I got out my notebook and wrote down the hour, the date, the place . . . And Mara, where was she now? She too had dropped out, *forever.* Strange how some enter one's life for just a moment or two, and then are gone, *forever.* And yet there is nothing accidental about such meetings.

Perhaps Mara had been sent to remind me that I would never be happy until I found Christine again . . .

A week later, at the home of a Hindu dancer, I was introduced to an extraordinarily beautiful Danish girl newly arrived from Copenhagen. She was decidedly not "my type," but she was ravishingly beautiful, no denying it. A sort of legendary Norse figure come to life. Naturally, everybody was courting her. I paid no obvious attention to her, although my eyes were constantly following her, until we were thrown together in the little room where the drinks were being served. By this time everybody, except the dancer, had had too much to drink. The Danish beauty was leaning against the wall with a glass in her hand. Her reserve had broken down. She had the air of one who was waiting to be mussed up. As I approached she said with a seductive grin: "So you're the man who writes those terrible books?" I didn't bother to reply. I put my glass down and closed in on her, kissing her blindly, passionately, savagely. She came out of the embrace pushing me violently away. She was not angry. On the contrary, I sensed that she was expecting me to repeat the attack. "Not here," she said aloud.

The Hindu girl had begun to dance; the guests politely took their places about the room. The Danish girl, whose name turned out to be Christine, led me into the kitchen on the pretext of making me a sandwich.

"You know I'm a married woman," she

said, almost immediately we were alone. "Yes, and I have two children, two beautiful children. Do you like children?"

"I like *you*," I said, giving her another embrace and kissing her hungrily.

"Would you marry me," she said, "if I were free?"

Just like that she popped it, without any preliminaries. I was so astonished that I said the only thing a man can say under the circumstances. I said Yes.

"Yes," I repeated, "I'd marry you tomorrow . . . Right now, if you say the word."

"Don't be so quick," she sallied, "I may take you at your word." This was said with such forthrightness that for an instant I was dead sober, almost frightened. "Oh, I'm not going to ask you to marry me immediately," she continued, observing my dismay. "I merely wanted to see if you were the marrying kind. My husband is dead. I have been a widow for over a year."

Those words had the effect of making me lecherous. Why had she come to Paris? Obviously to enjoy herself. Hers was the typical cold seductive charm of the North-

ern woman in whom prudery and las-
civiousness battle for supremacy. I knew
she wanted me to talk love. Say anything
you like, do anything you like, but use the
language of love—the glamorous, romantic, sentimental words which conceal the
ugly, naked reality of the sexual assault.

I placed my hand squarely over her cunt,
which was steaming like manure under her
dress, and said: "*Christine,* what a wonderful name! Only a woman like you could
own such a romantic name. It makes me
think of icy fjords, of fir trees dripping with
wet snow. If you were a tree I would pull
you up by the roots. I'd carve my initials
in your trunk . . ." I rattled off more silly
nonsense, all the while clutching her firmly,
pushing my fingers into her gluey crack. I
don't know how far it would have gone,
there in the kitchen, if our hostess had not
interrupted us. She was a lascivious bitch,
too. I had to mush it up with both of them
at the same time. Out of politeness we
finally went back to the big room to watch
the Hindu girl's performance. We stood
well back from the others, in a dark corner.
I had my arm around Christine; with my

143

free hand I did what I could with the other.

The party came to an abrupt end because of a fist fight between two drunken Americans. In the confusion Christine left with the jaded-looking Count who had brought her to the place. Fortunately I got her address before leaving.

When I got home I gave Carl a glowing account of the affair. He was all a-twitter. We must invite her for dinner—the sooner the better. He would ask a friend of his to come, a new one, whom he had met at the Cirque Médrano. She was an acrobat, he said. I didn't believe a word of it, but I grinned and said it would be fine.

The evening came. Carl had prepared the dinner and, as usual, had bought the most expensive wines. The acrobat arrived first. She was alert, intelligent, spry, with cute diminutive features which, because of her frizzy coiffure, made her look somewhat like a Pomeranian dog. She was one of those happy-go-lucky souls who fuck on sight. Carl didn't rave about her to the extent he usually did when he made a new find. He was genuinely relieved, however, that he had found someone to replace the morose Eliane.

"How does she look to you?" he asked me on the side. "Do you think she'll do? Not too bad, is she?" Then, as an afterthought—"By the way, Eliane seems quite stuck on you. Why don't you look her up? She's not a bad lay, I can vouch for that. You don't have to waste time on preliminaries; just whisper a few kind words and push her over. She's got a cunt that works like a suction pump . . ."

With this he beckoned to Corinne, his acrobatic friend, to join us. "Turn around," he said, "I want to show him your ass." He rubbed his hand over her rump appraisingly. "Feel *that,* Joey," he said. "It's like velvet, what?"

I was just in the act of following his suggestion when there was a knock at the door. "That must be *your* cunt," said Carl, going to the door and opening it. At sight of Christine he let out a howl and, throwing his arms around her, he dragged her into the room, exclaiming—"She's marvelous, marvelous! Why didn't you tell me how beautiful she was?"

I thought he would go off his nut with admiration. He danced around the room and clapped his hands like a child. "Oh, Joey, Joey," he said, fairly licking his chops in anticipation, "She's *wonderful*. She's the best cunt you ever dug up!"

Christine caught the word cunt. "What does it mean?" she asked.

"It means you're beautiful, dazzling, radiant," said Carl, holding her hands ecstatically. His eyes were moist as a puppy's.

Christine's English was almost elementary; Corinne knew even less. So we spoke French. As an appetizer, we had some Alsatian wine. Someone put on a record, whereupon Carl began to sing in a loud piercing voice, his face red as a beet, his lips wet, his eyes gleaming. Every now and then he would go up to Corinne and give her a wet smack on the mouth—to show that he hadn't forgotten her. But everything he said was addressed to Christine.

"Christine!" he would say, caressing her arm, stroking her like a cat. *"Christine! What a magical name!"* (Actually he detested the name; he used to say that it was a stupid name, fit for a cow or a spavined horse.) "Let me think," and he would roll his eyes heavenward, as if struggling to capture the precise metaphor. "It's like fragile lace in moonlight. No, not moonlight—*twilight*. Anyway, it's fragile, delicate, like your soul . . . Give me another drink, someone. I can think of better images than that."

Christine, in her down-to-earth way, interrupted the performance by inquiring if dinner were soon ready. Carl pretended to be shocked. "How can a beautiful creature like you think of food at such a moment?" he exclaimed.

But Corinne was hungry too. We sat down, Carl still red as a beet. He shifted his watery gaze from one to the other, as if uncertain which one to lick first. He was definitely in a mood to lick them from head to foot. After he had taken a few mouthfuls, he got up and slobbered over Corinne. Then, as if he had a dose of catnip, he sidled around to Christine and went to work on her. The effect was pleasing but left them slightly dazed. They must have wondered just how the evening would terminate.

As yet I hadn't touched Christine. I was curious to observe her behavior—how she talked, how she laughed, how she ate and drank. Carl kept filling the glasses, as if it were lemonade we were drinking. Christine seemed shy, I thought, but the wine was soon to take effect. It was not long before I felt a hand on my leg, squeezing it. I grasped it and put it between my legs. She drew it away, as if frightened.

Carl now began plying her with questions about Copenhagen, about her children, about her married life. (He had forgotten that her husband was dead.) Suddenly, apropos of nothing, he looked at her with a malicious grin, and said: "*Ecoute, petite,* what I'd like to know is this—does he give you a good fuck now and then?"

Christine went scarlet. Looking him in the eye, she answered stonily: "*Il est mort, mon mari.*"

Anyone else would have been mortified. Not Carl. He rose to his feet with a natural, good-humored expression and, going over to her, he kissed her chastely on the brow. "*Je t'aime,*" he said, and trotted back to his seat. A moment later he was babbling about spinach and how good it tasted raw.

There is something about Northern people I don't understand. I've never met one, male or female, whom I could really warm up to. I don't mean, in voicing this, that Christine's presence acted as a pall. On the contrary, the evening rolled along like a well-oiled machine. Dinner over, Carl moved his acrobat over to the divan. I lay down on the rug with Christine, in the next room. It was a bit of a struggle at first, but once I had gotten her legs open and the juice flowing, she went at it with gusto. After a few spasms she began to weep. She was weeping over her dead husband, so she confessed. I couldn't make it out. I felt like saying, "Why bring *that* up now?" I endeavored to find out what it was, precisely, that she was thinking of with respect to her departed husband. To my amazement, she said: "What would he think of me if he could see me lying here on the floor with you?" That struck me as so ridiculous that I felt like spanking her. An unholy desire possessed me to make her do something which would warrant a true display of shame and remorse.

Just then I heard Carl get up to go to the bathroom. I called to him to join us in a drink. "Wait a minute," he said, "that bitch is bleeding like a stuck pig." When he came out of the bathroom I told him, in English, to try his luck with Christine. Whereupon I excused myself and went to the bathroom. When I returned, Christine was still lying on the floor, smoking a cigarette. Carl was lying beside her, gently trying to pry her legs open. She lay there cool as a cucumber, her legs crossed, a blank expression on her face. I poured some more drinks and went into the other room to chat with Corinne. She too was lying back with a cigarette between her lips, ready, I suppose, for another bout if anyone happened along. I sat beside her and talked a blue streak in order to give Carl time to get his end in.

Just when I thought that everything was going well Christine suddenly popped into the room. In the darkness she stumbled against the divan. I caught hold of her and pulled her over beside Corinne. In a moment Carl also came in and flung himself on the divan. Everybody was silent. We shifted about, trying to make ourselves comfortable. In pawing around, my hand touched a bare breast. It was round and firm, the nipple taut and tempting. I closed my mouth over it. It was Christine's perfume that I recognized. Moving my head up to seek her mouth, I felt a hand sliding into my fly. As I slid my tongue into her mouth I shifted slightly to permit Corinne to extricate my cock. In a moment I felt her warm breath on it. While she nibbled away I clutched Christine passionately, biting her lips, her tongue, her throat. She seemed to be in an unusual state of passion, making the queerest grunts and spasmodic movements of the body. With her arms around my neck she held me in a vise; her tongue had thickened, as though swollen with blood. I struggled to get my prick free of Corinne's molten furnace of a mouth, but in vain. Gently I tried to wiggle it free, but she kept after it like a fish, securing it with her teeth.

Meanwhile Christine was twitching more violently, as though in the throes of an orgasm. I managed to extricate my arm, which had been pinned under her back, and slid my hand down her torso. Just below the waist I felt something hard; it was covered with hair. I dug my fingers into it. "Hey, it's *me*," said Carl, pulling his head away. With that Christine started pulling me away from Corinne, but Corinne refused to let go. Carl now threw himself on Christine who was beside herself. I was lying so that I was now able to tickle her ass while Carl dug away at her. I thought she would go mad, from the way she was wriggling about and moaning and gibbering.

Suddenly it was over. At once Christine bounded out of the bed and made for the bathroom. For a moment or two the three of us were silent. Then, as if we had been hit in the same crazy place, we burst into peals of laughter. Carl laughed loudest of all—one of his crazy laughs which threatened never to come to an end.

We were still laughing when the bathroom door was suddenly flung open. There stood Christine in a blaze of light, her face flaming red, demanding angrily to know where her wraps were.

"You're disgusting," she yelled. "Let me out of here!"

Carl made an attempt to soothe her ruffled feelings but I cut it short by saying, "Let her go if she wants to." I didn't even get up to look for her things. I heard Carl say something to her in a muffled voice, and then I heard Christine's angry voice saying, "Leave me alone—you're a filthy pig!" With that the door slammed and she was gone.

"That's your Scandinavian beauty for you," I said.

"Yah, yah," muttered Carl, pacing back and forth with head down. "It's bad, it's bad," he mumbled.

"What's bad?" I said. "Don't be a fool! We gave her the time of her life."

He began to titter in crazy fashion. "What if she had the clap?" he said, and made a dash for the bathroom, where he noisily gargled his throat. "Listen, Joey," he shouted, spitting out a mouthful, "what do you suppose made her so angry? Because we laughed so hard?"

"They're all like that," said Corinne. "*La pudeur.*"

"I'm hungry," said Carl. "Let's sit down and have another meal. Maybe she'll change her mind and come back." He mumbled something to himself, then added, as if doing a sum—"It doesn't make sense."

—Henry Miller
New York City,
May, 1940.
Rewritten in Big Sur, May, 1956.